ORTEGA MAFIA – THE CONSIGLIERE

A DARK MAFIA ROMANCE

STELLA ANDREWS

Copyrighted Material
Copyright © Stella Andrews 2023
Stella Andrews has asserted her rights under the Copyright, Designs and Patents Act 1988 to be identified as the Author of this work.
This book is a work of fiction and except in the case of historical fact, any resemblance to actual persons, living or dead, is purely coincidental.
All rights reserved. No part of this book may be reproduced or transmitted in any form without written permission of the author, except by a reviewer who may quote brief passages for review purposes only.

18+ This book is for adults only. If you are easily shocked and not a fan of sexual content, then move away now.

18+

NEWSLETTER

Sign up to my newsletter and download a free eBook

stellaandrews.com

ORTEGA MAFIA

The Consigliere

The devil dances on the sabbath while the innocent rest.

My stepmother and her deranged lover stole our business.
The Ortega Mafia is ours by birth but they have other ideas.

With the help of my two brothers, it's time to steal it back and I have a secret weapon.

Abigail Kensington.

Billionaire's daughter and Washington princess.
The perfect woman who is definitely out of my league.
A woman my target is obsessed with. The one woman he never had and settled for my stepmother instead.

I am a master at exploiting weakness and will make the pampered princess an offer she can't refuse.

I will use her, probably abuse her and ruin her, in my thirst for revenge.

She is a pawn in my wicked game of chess, and I play to win.

I will destroy lives and corrupt souls all in the name of victory, and they won't know what hit them.

It's time to gain the upper hand and take charge of our destiny.
The Ortega Mafia is ours, and nobody will ever get in the way of that.

Buckle up for a dark, twisted ride of family secrets, lies, and revenge. Somewhere in the middle of the mayhem, a love story evolves that has a very hard beginning.

Fans of Dark Mafia Romance will love Ortega Mafia.

Books in the series.

The Enforcer
　The Consigliere
　The Don

PROLOGUE

ABIGAIL AGE 16

I can tell my mother is nervous. She has a nervous habit of twisting her wedding band that sits beneath the largest solitaire diamond when she's anxious.

Her manicured nails gleam with fresh polish and her perfectly styled hair is cemented in place by a can of spray. Her clothes are fresh off the designer's drawing board and the Hermes purse on her lap isn't even on sale yet. To anyone looking in from the outside, she has it all.

As she sits straight-backed and rigid, her emotions firmly disguised, she glances out of the window at the passing scenery as if that's all she needs to think about.

My attention shifts to the man sitting beside her, his attention dominated by his phone. Fresh texts flash up on repeat, and he appears engrossed in them.

Jared Kensington. Washington billionaire. A man who desires control and is always searching for the next investment to toss on the ever-growing pile of wealth this family enjoys.

I glance down and note how neatly folded my hands are in my lap. Like my mother, my back is straight and rigid, my legs crossed at my ankles and my own Chanel suit crease free, having only just been liberated from the store. The matching purse rests on the plush leather seat by my side, holding nothing more than a lipstick and my cell. I am expected to sit in silence and yet many questions are begging to be heard because there must be a good reason why we are attending the party of mom's childhood friend, Claire Bachini.

We made the flight in my father's private jet and are now heading toward the home of a woman who mom lost touch with years ago. I believe it was only due to a chance encounter in Washington that we are here at all, and that is why the questions won't go away.

Mom hates reminding of her past. The one when daddy wasn't in it and the fact he's accompanying us also raises questions because in my entire life, my father has never attended any event that doesn't benefit his business in some way.

I'm curious what Mr. Bachini does for a living and the only information I have is what I discovered online, and that raises more questions than answers.

I would ask them, any normal person would, but I know better than that. Don't ask, just wait to be told. That's always been the case in my relationship with my parents and so I glance out of the window, much like my mother, and wait for the truth to reveal itself.

I'm still waiting as the car pulls through large iron gates and heads up a sweeping drive before coming to a stop outside a huge red brick house. Unlike our own white marbled palace, this one appears small, crowded and stuck in the past.

Then again, not many homes measure up to ours, and I hate myself for even comparing them. We live a life many never imagine, and I'm guessing to most people, the Bachinis are doing extremely well for themselves.

Mom's sigh escapes before she can check it and my father snaps, "One hour should be enough. I'm sure you can manage that."

Mom nods, a pained expression on her face, and glances sharply in my direction.

"Sit up, Abigail, your posture is appalling these days. Don't they teach you anything at that insanely expensive school we send you to?"

Her mouth tightens in disapproval and I loathe that I sit more upright, holding my breath, yearning for the tiniest bit of approval in those sparkling green eyes.

My father flicks an irritated glance my way and then lowers his voice, addressing me directly.

"They have a son. Mario."

My heart thumps at the distaste on his face as he says with a sigh. "Keep away from him."

Mom snaps. "I told you we should have left Abigail at home."

He rolls his eyes. "They specifically asked her to be here."

Mom shakes her head. "Since when did you care what other people think?"

For some reason, my father lowers his eyes and I note the pulse throbbing in his jaw indicating he's uncomfortable. I've seen that look before, recently in fact. It struck me as curious then and for some reason I'm uneasy as he peers up and regards me with a guilty expression.

"One hour." He almost mumbles and then the conversation stops as the car grinds to a halt on the gravel path and the door is opened by a man who looks as if he eats humans for breakfast.

He says nothing and as we exit the car, I gaze around me at a place that makes me shiver. There is something sinister about this house. I can't put my finger on it, but I *feel* it. It's surrounding me and sets my heart thumping, and not in a good way.

The bear like man guides us toward the open front door and I hear laughter coming from inside.

It's obviously a party, because there is music accompanied by the general hum of conversation provided by several voices. I stare in amazement at the uniformed servers weaving their way in and out of the guests with silver platters laden with champagne and canapés.

Before we can make it a few feet inside, a woman swoops down on my mother with her arms outstretched.

"Anna, darling. How wonderful you could make it."

I notice my mother flinch before contact and as they air kiss, I don't miss her friend's piercing gaze settle on me and if anything, she appears to be assessing me.

She pulls back and purrs, "This must be your beautiful daughter, Abigail."

Mom nods and says sharply, "Abigail, where are your manners?"

I paste a bright smile on my face and say politely, "It's a pleasure to meet you, Mrs. Bachini."

I sense there is something happening I can't work out as she stares at me with an intensity that makes me a little uncomfortable.

She is joined by a man who is equally creepy, and his expression is much the same as he stares at me with a hunger that causes me to step back a little.

"Jared, Anna, I'm so glad you could make it."

The man says loudly, causing a few guests standing nearby to glance up with an expression of curiosity. I'm guessing this is her husband, Sam Bachini and I shiver inside as I sense there is something not quite right about this man.

If anything, it appears we are the star attraction and I wonder about that.

Mrs. Bachini glances behind her and says loudly, "Mario, come and say hi to our guests."

I'm not sure if it's my imagination or not, but my father

moves in front of me as a guy who makes my flesh creep steps into view.

Their son obviously inherited his parents' piercing gaze as he runs it the length of me with a hunger that sets me on edge. He appears to be a little older than me and is possibly the most unattractive man I have ever met. His hair is greased back, and his eyes are narrow. He stands tall and thin, and his suit hangs off his body as if it would rather not touch him at all. His pale skin and dark shifty eyes are a serious turnoff, and the way he licks his lips as he stares at me puts me on edge.

He holds out his hand and I have no choice but to take it and as his clammy hand closes around mine, he raises it to his lips and just the touch of those wet lips on my skin makes me want to snatch my hand away and wipe it on the drapes because this guy is seriously disgusting.

"It's a pleasure to meet you, Miss. Kensington."

I nod, words escaping me because the pleasure is definitely not mine.

I make to take my hand away, but he grips on tight and it's a little awkward as my father pulls me roughly back and says firmly, "I believe we have business to discuss, Sam."

I glance up in surprise and register the resignation on my mother's face as Mrs. Bachini smiles almost victoriously. "Come, Anna. Let's go and catch up and leave the men to talk."

She turns to her son. "Mario, perhaps you could entertain Abigail."

I don't appreciate his sly look as he stares at my chest and thank God for my father because he snaps, "Abigail will be fine with Anna. We don't allow her to mix with the opposite sex —ever."

If anything, I note the narrowing eyes of our host, which is quickly replaced with a false smile.

"Of course."

Mrs. Bachini says quickly, "Perhaps she would prefer to spend time with our two daughters instead."

I glance up in surprise as Mrs. Bachini points out two girls who appear to be the same age as me, but my father says firmly, "She stays with my wife."

I cast a curious gaze in their direction and note the two almost identical girls who look nothing like the Bachinis. They are both extremely pretty blondes with the most astonishing blue eyes and yet when I peer closer, I note the animosity in one of the girl's eyes as she looks my way. It unnerves me a little, especially when I notice her sister staring at Mario with a contemplative expression. There is something extremely weird about this family and for once I am keen to remain in the dark because if I never see any of them again, I will die happy.

* * *

EXACTLY ONE HOUR LATER, my father reappears and rescues us from the most excruciating conversation with Mrs. Bachini and as we make to leave, I can tell my father is extremely unhappy. Angry in fact, and I wonder what the meeting was about.

I note the concern in my mother's eyes as she shares a look with her husband and then we are saying our goodbyes before I can process what's happening.

As we make to leave, I catch sight of their son Mario standing beside one of the pretty girls and it makes me shiver inside. The expression of hatred on her face is solely directed at me, but it's Mario's expression that scares me the most. It's as if he wants to devour me and what I register in his eyes is a promise.

There is something very disturbing about our visit today and I'm almost certain the reason for it concerns the two of us, and I can't get out of here quickly enough.

CHAPTER 1

MATTEO

FIVE YEARS LATER

The door opens, and Cesare, my consigliere, enters the room with a wry smile.

"Boss." He nods with respect, and I wave to the chair set before my desk.

"How did it go?"

I reach for my lighter and flick the flame against the finest Cuban cigar, taking a deep drag and then clipping the end, before replacing it in the box.

Cesare barks out a laugh.

"I thought you gave up."

"I have." I grin as he settles back in his seat and shakes his head.

"It never ceases to amaze me how gullible rich kids are."

"So, he took the bait."

Cesare nods, his eyes glittering with devilish mirth.

"A private booth and champagne on the house to celebrate

his birthday. Invites for ten of his friends and a complimentary lap dance."

"He would be a fool to refuse."

I glance at the photo on my phone and consider the beauty staring back at me.

"And his girlfriend? Will she be joining him?"

"What do you think?"

Abigail Kensington. Billionaire's daughter and, by all accounts, the love of Mario Bachini's life. The one woman he never had and desired more for it. Currently hooked up with Jefferson Stevenson, the son of a powerful Judge and friend of her parents. They are obviously orchestrating a union between their families and Abigail is the pawn in their game, which is a coincidence because she's also the pawn in mine.

We move onto other business, but I keep the phone with her picture by my side, glancing at it occasionally and familiarizing myself with an important piece of the puzzle. I will use her, probably abuse her and ruin her and it will all be because I am thirsty for revenge.

* * *

Later that evening, I watch from my office as Jefferson arrives with nine of his friends. There is not one girl among them which tells me everything I need to know.

The booth is positioned exactly at the right angle for my security cameras to film every detail, and I wait for the inevitable with a cut glass of whiskey in my hand and the unlit cigar in the other.

Show time.

At first the group is rowdy but not out of line and enjoys the endless champagne I ply them with. Rich kids never question a gift. They believe it's their right and probably think my establishment is sucking up to them for their business.

My manager is under instruction to make this a night to remember, but it won't be for their benefit. No, it's purely for mine to drive my kill into my sights.

Sherrie, one of my most skilled lap dancers, sways across to the booth and proceeds to do what she does best. She gyrates, titillates, and provokes and only when she asks who the birthday boy is, does she strike.

I watch her straddle Jefferson, who appears to be loving every second of it, and he soon has his hands over her as she sucks on his neck.

His friends encourage him on and as she drops to her knees and unzips his pants, their cheers can be heard over the loud music.

The camera zooms in on Jefferson's face and from the look of it he's enjoying every minute and when Sherrie pulls back and shifts onto his lap, there's no mistaking what's happening now.

He thrusts up inside her and my camera catches every sordid minute of it and when they finish, it's to cheers and requests for the same. I make a fist when he takes out a roll of dollars and slips it into her mouth, slapping her on the ass as she leaves. Fucking creep, at this moment I want to waste the prick myself, but that wouldn't help my plan.

As they congratulate their friend, another waitress stops by with a silver tray lined with ten rows of cocaine and they need no further encouragement to inhale their lines like the good little rich kids they are.

More lap dances involve their friends and it's not far off a fucking orgy and then Sherrie returns and fastens a leather collar around Jefferson's neck and leads him away to a private room.

I switch cameras and record the entire sordid freak show as she humiliates him by whipping his ass, caning his legs and making him crawl around the room before eating her pussy.

Job done, humiliation complete and as I press send, I wait for the recipient to beat down my door.

* * *

ONE HOUR LATER, the fun really begins.

I study her arrival with interest. The car draws up outside and my uniformed guard on the door opens it and a long shapely leg exits first, followed by a woman who could grace any Paris runway.

Her silver dress moves independently of her, dusting her knees as she towers on the highest heels that give me an instant hard on.

She straightens up and tosses her sandy hair across her shoulder and glances up at the name above my club, her lips set in a grim line and her vivid green eyes flashing as she nods her thanks to the guard who holds the rope aside to let her pass.

Cesare is waiting just inside the door and approaches her with a respectful smile and as he guides her past the door leading into the club, I prepare myself for battle.

Mere seconds later the door opens, and she enters my office, trying to appear unconcerned, but I already sense her emotion.

"Mr. Ortega, I presume."

She glances past me, and I notice her skin pale as she witnesses her current boyfriend fucking one of my staff doggy style.

For a moment she falters, and her dark stormy eyes sparkle with unshed tears.

"Please take a seat, Miss. Kensington."

She drops into the seat opposite me, and I hand her a glass of champagne, causing her to flinch.

"Are we celebrating, Mr. Ortega?"

She glances back to the screen and her lips tighten as she witnesses what her boyfriend does in his spare time.

"Of course."

I sit behind my desk and smile, nodding to the monitor and saying huskily, "Have you seen enough?"

"No." She fixes her eyes on the screen and raises the glass to her lips and for once I'm surprised by a reaction. I thought she'd be inconsolable, tearful, and hysterical. Not this cold fury and desire to watch every sordid second of her boyfriend's infidelity.

She doesn't tear her eyes from the scene as she says conversationally, "So, what's this about? Why send this to me with an invitation to meet you?"

"Because I have a business proposition for you."

"I'm not in business."

She cringes as Jefferson slaps Sherrie's ass hard.

"I beg to differ, Miss. Kensington."

"You know nothing about me."

I'm impressed with the fire inside her and I say slowly, "Let me refresh your memory, then. You are in the business of being set up as a trophy wife. Your husband to be is currently starring in his own porn movie that could end up in the public domain if you choose to walk away."

Her eyes flick away from the screen, and I almost flinch under her derisive gaze.

"What do I care? Publish it. It's his shit to deal with, not mine."

She raises her glass to the screen and then to me and for some reason that impresses me more than anything so far. She has a fiery spark in her and I kind of love my women like that and so I bark out a laugh and then fix her with my deadliest glare that definitely gets her attention.

"Miss. Kensington. I don't believe you have understood how serious this situation is. Jefferson's father is Judge Stevenson.

The most powerful judge in the state who is currently on your father's radar as your future father-in-law. You have entered into an agreement that your engagement will be announced at the beginning of the summer, allowing for endless parties and social gatherings to celebrate that fact."

I lean forward and stare at her hard. "In doing so, your father makes the perfect marriage for his daughter, to the man who is tipped to follow in his father's footsteps. Your future is guaranteed and yet one leak on the internet would have Jefferson up on drugs and prostitution charges, not to mention the scandal that would destroy his family."

I lean back and smirk. "By association, your family would be affected. The scandal would create a wide berth around them. Social invitations would dry up, business deals withdrawn and socially you would be humiliated and ridiculed. Need I go on."

She sighs and studies her fingernails as if I'm a mild irritant that she needs to deal with before pulling her boyfriend back in line and then straightening the gilded mirror they live their life staring into.

So, I go in for the kill.

"I need you to ditch Jefferson and agree to be my girlfriend."

"You are kidding me."

Her eyes widen and I nod, feeling extremely smug about this.

"You see, every kid goes off the rails at least once in their life and this will be brushed under the Persian rug as yours. Your parents will make excuses that you are overseas for the summer, educating yourself and helping build an orphanage, or something along those charitable lines. Jefferson will receive a copy of this recording with instruction to play along or face his future blowing up in his face. You help me with a problem I have and we're all happy when you return home and take up where you left off. It's a small price to pay for a few weeks of rebellion, wouldn't you agree, Miss. Kensington?"

She stares at me as if I'm the Grim Reaper and then her gaze flicks back to the screen as her boyfriend pulls on his trousers and then beckons Sherrie to sit on his lap, proceeding to suck her breasts as she fists his hair.

To my surprise, Abigail sighs heavily.

"What do I have to do?"

"I told you. Play the part of my girlfriend and come home and meet the family. That's all I ask."

"But why?"

"I have my reasons."

The last thing I'm revealing is who will be there. I am looking forward to that more than anything.

The fact this woman is eye candy of the sexiest kind has already re-written the contract from the one I first had in mind.

Yes, Abigail Kensington is a challenge. Mario failed, but I never do and as my girlfriend, I expect her to fulfill the job description in every way. When Mario Bachini realizes I'm fucking the love of his life, it will push him to the edge and it's good to know that I'm the man he'll find waiting there to push him off.

Abigail sets the glass on the desk and stands, flicking one hard look toward the screen.

"You have a deal, Mr. Ortega. Text me the details. I've seen enough. I'll be your girlfriend, but in name only. I'm not my boyfriend, I don't cheat, and I don't sleep around. Whatever your reason for staging this…" she waves her hand at the screen. "event, is not my concern. What does concern me is my future and if that is with or without Jefferson, I have yet to decide."

She tosses her hair behind her like every rich princess I have ever met, and the way she looks down on me tells me exactly what she thinks of me. If anything, I'm glad about that because it will make my job a much easier one. Dominate the princess and bring her in line, wiping that regal smirk from her face and crushing her soul.

Once again, I light the cigar and prepare to ruin Jefferson Stevenson's life along with his girlfriend's and the people I detest most in the world.

Mario Bachini and Diana Ortega, my wicked stepmother. It will be cruel, vindictive, and glorious and at the end of it, I will walk over their broken souls victorious.

CHAPTER 2

ABIGAIL

I'm still shaking. Not that you'd know it because I've been trained to disguise my emotions, but that was something else. *He* was something else and I don't believe I will ever get over being in the same room as that man.

Matteo Ortega. His name graces the club I just left and if ever I met evil, it was there in his office. I knew as soon as I entered and cast one look at the man that I was way out of my depth.

I'm still processing what happened in that room as the cab driver says gruffly, "Where are you going?"

I open my mouth to direct him back to the club where my friends are waiting, but for some reason, I direct him to a different destination entirely.

His raised brow almost causes me to change my mind and I glare at him with a defiance that even surprises me.

"Are you sure, honey?"

He scratches his head and I almost back out, but I am too fired up to consider the consequences of my actions.

"I'm sure."

I look away before he can register the fear in my eyes

because what the hell am I doing? I must be insane, but after what I saw in that office, I am no longer in control of my sanity.

My heart is pounding, and I try desperately to get my breathing under control because what am I even thinking?

That I'm aware of this place is shocking enough, but the fact I'm actually thinking of going tells me I've lost leave of my senses.

I'm still unsure why I have such an overwhelming need to go there, but there was something so deliciously sinister about what just happened and it left my morality in shreds at my feet after what Jefferson did to me tonight.

I almost can't think of him right now. Witnessing him with a whore, obviously enjoying every second of it, made me want to hurl. He was nothing like the polite, reserved man my parents have arranged a marriage with. Respectable, intelligent and hungry for power. The man I saw was entirely different and I couldn't tear my eyes away from the scene playing out before my disbelieving eyes.

My phone buzzes and I see a text from Clarice, my friend.

> **CLARICE**
>
> Hey, babe. Where are you? We want to leave for Jimmy Johnson's

> **ABI**
>
> Sorry, got a migraine. If anyone asks, I was with you all night. You know how my parents hate me being out on my own.

> **CLARICE**
> Sure. You can count on me. Where are you heading?

> **ABI**
> Pool house.

I hold my breath, hoping she accepts my explanation. Clarice knows the pool house is my bolt hole. The place I go when I want to be alone and I'm hoping my story checks out now.

She texts back.

> **CLARICE**
> If you need company, I'll meet you there

> **ABI**
> It's ok. I'm not good company right now. I'll pop an Advil and watch a chick flick. I'll be fine in the morning.

> **CLARICE**
> Sorry babe. Bad luck. I'll call you tomorrow

As the conversation ends, I exhale slowly. Thank God I lead a sheltered life. Even Clarice won't doubt my story because when has Abigail Kensington ever done anything not scripted in her parent's handbook? No, I'm the good girl. The pretty princess who does everything she is told to do. Dress respectfully, fix my hair a certain way. Exercise, speak and even read books that are chosen for me. I am not allowed my own mind at all, and my entire life is controlled by my parents. Even my future has been determined by them. Marry Jefferson Stevenson and help him with his political aspirations. An arranged marriage that offers no room for argument.

Engagement announcement this summer. Wedding the next. Then honeymoon in Europe before producing three children and playing the trophy wife. I've been trained for this my entire life, which is why in one rash moment of rebellion I am heading to a place that good girls would run from in horror.

The Banned Room.

The cab pulls up outside the darkened façade of an establishment that is whispered about amid giggles at sleepover parties. Inside those dark doors is a world of depravation that made our eyes widen in disbelief and fear cloud our hearts. It's a world away from the elite and yet after what I saw tonight, it's closer than I thought and, rather than being repulsed by it, I was intrigued.

I thrust some dollars into the cab driver's hands, and he says with a sigh, "Are you sure about this? I'll wait for a few minutes if you change your mind."

"I won't."

I slam the door behind me and take a deep breath because for the first time in her life, Abigail Kensington is doing something for herself, that was her own decision and is guaranteed to end the life of her parents if they ever discovered where she was.

My heart thumps as I walk with purpose toward the black door, the red words above adding drama to the place. The Banned Room makes my heart lurch, my knees shake and the wet heat inside me to bubble up because I must be a freak. There was something so exhilarating about Jefferson with that woman, but it wasn't him I was picturing in my mind at all. It was the enigmatic man observing me so keenly from across the desk that fired up my libido and scrambled my mind.

Matteo Ortega.

From the moment I sat down, I was aware of him. His chiseled dark good looks and heavy dark eyes, loaded with intensity that stripped my breath away.

The way he spoke in a husky, slow voice that crawled through my mind, promising danger at his hands. The lazy way his eyes dragged across my body, scorching my skin with one lust-filled gaze. There was his tanned skin that peered out from under his black silk shirt, unbuttoned low enough to reveal the dark intricate ink that nestled among the smattering of dark hair on his chest. His flashing eyes and the way he rubbed his finger against his lips made me weak with desire.

As I watched Jefferson, I was only conscious of Matteo, and when he revealed the reason for the meeting, my heart leaped at the danger I now found myself in.

He wants me to be his girlfriend.

It took my breath away and more for my benefit than his I issued my demands because even if my thoughts have betrayed me, my head is still firmly in charge.

I push the door open with an anticipation that causes me to shiver. What is going to happen inside these walls? Will I walk out the same person I am now, or will I tumble foolishly into the darkness and never find my way out again?

The red lights add drama to every footstep I make as I tread the red carpet leading me past mirrors lining the hallway. At the end is a desk where a woman sits regarding my approach with curiosity more than anything else.

She is dressed in a black corset, her breasts spilling over the top and her ruby red lips part in a smile as she says brightly, "How can I help you, honey?"

I am so nervous and say in a whisper, "I, well, um..."

She smiles softly. "You're curious, perhaps?"

I nod and she leans forward and whispers, "I should tell you to spin on your heels and head back the way you came. This isn't the right place for a lady like you."

"But–" I feel crushed because now I'm here I want to see what's inside so badly and my heart sinks when she shakes her head. "I can't let you in."

"Why not?"

I find my voice and she says gently, "I don't know what you've heard, but there are rules for places like this. If I let you inside, you're fair game."

"Why?"

I'm curious and she points to my neck. "Firstly, you're not wearing a collar which tells the men in there and some women that you're available."

"I am."

I say it so softly she raises her eyes. "Are you sure about that?"

I will be extremely disappointed if I fail now, so I say with some urgency, "I want one night when I lose myself. I have never been able to do that before. I'm observed, controlled and manipulated and this is my one chance of freedom. Let me experience something I never will again. Please."

I almost think she pities me and my heart leaps when she nods.

"Don't say I didn't warn you."

She taps on her screen before saying briskly, "Type in your details. Make them up if it's easier. Nobody gives a fuck anyway. There's only one thing they'll want from you, honey, and you should be prepared for that."

Before I can change my mind, I type in a false name and address and make up a phone number.

Then she reaches under the desk and fastens a band to my wrist.

"Here. Wear this and enjoy. If you don't want to do anything, tell them. Nobody can force you into anything in this club. If you'd rather just watch, that's fine too but be prepared for more than one person's interest. This could be the night of your dreams or your worst nightmare. You have been warned."

She presses something and the door swings open behind her and as the sultry music wafts toward me, I shiver as I step inside.

CHAPTER 3

MATTEO

*J*efferson returns to his friends like a conquering hero. From the animated conversation, I can tell he's relaying every sordid second of his encounter with Sherrie and his friends appear impressed. They slap him on the back and hang off his words, and I itch to wipe that smug grin off his face with my fist.

Cesare heads back to the office and for a moment we both stare at the group of privileged kids who have never done a hard day's work in their life and Cesare says roughly, "I can't wait to see that smug shit's smile wiped off his face."

"Agreed."

Sighing, I grab my jacket and shrug it on, before turning to Cesare and grinning, "It's time to greet our guests."

We head out of my office and make the short walk to the door at the end that leads into my club, and even though Cesare walks beside me, it's Abigail Kensington who follows me there. I am intrigued by her. She was nothing like I expected her to be, and I'm surprised by that. That alone piques my interest because I am never surprised by a person's character. I have an ability to sum them up with one conversation and a dark look, but not her. Far from being the pampered princess I gave her credit for, she is way more layered than that.

"Did you put eyes on our departing guest?"

For some reason, I need to know that happened and Cesare nods. "Kris and Harry. They followed the cab and are under instruction not to let her out of their sight."

"Good."

My heart settles now she is protected, although that's a fucking joke because I am her biggest threat and nothing can protect that woman from what I have in mind for her.

My security guard opens the door to the club with a respectful nod and as soon as we step inside, the stench of alcohol and depravation hits me.

I'm home.

Curious eyes follow us as we make our way through the club, my soldiers falling into line to give us an unrestricted path to our destination. Men fear me, women want me, and I can't ever remember it being any different. However, there has only ever been one woman I let inside my heart, and she rewarded me by screwing my two brothers before marrying our father. I never thought I'd recover from that, but what's left is a white-hot fury that drives my revenge. Abigail will help me with that, and Jefferson is the insurance policy I drew up to get me what I want.

We reach his table and I note my girls draped across his friends like fashion accessories. As we stop at the table, the girls sit a little straighter and pout in my direction, but they never interest me.

Where's the fun of a woman giving it up freely? I like my women curious, slightly afraid, and fresh from the wrapper. Subsequently, my sex life is controlled and indulged infrequently. Chance encounters that end up with their lips wrapped around my cock or bent over my desk.

Usually, women who flock to my club to taste a bad boy on

an unexpected night out with their friends. They accept my champagne and adore my attention and when I make my choice, we retreat to my private room at the club. I treat them like whores out of revenge for the biggest one of them all and as I ruin them, I picture her traitorous face in place of theirs.

Emotion only knocked on my door once and now that door is locked to it. I will never allow a woman inside again because that only leads to damnation.

Drunken eyes stare at our arrival and I smile politely. "Gentlemen. I trust you found everything to your liking."

Jefferson nods smugly and rubs Sherrie's arm with an ownership that doesn't go unnoticed.

"Perfect" he grins, with all the smug satisfaction of the cat who got the cream, and his friends nod their thanks as they enjoy the attention of the girls on their laps and at their feet, all wearing scraps of fabric that barely cover their modesty.

"May I have a private word, Mr. Stevenson?"

The air goes still, and the light mood is extinguished like a dancing flame against the breeze.

Sherrie shifts off his lap, signaling the end to the evening and as she moves away, the other girls follow, leaving the guys with a sense of bewilderment that things have changed so fast.

My men move behind Jefferson, and I turn on my heel and head back the way I came, knowing that my men will ensure he is sitting in my office within the next five minutes.

We cut through the club like the sword of Damocles, which means something terrible is going to happen. That what looks like an enviable life, a life of wealth, a life of power, a life of luxury is, in fact, fraught with anxiety, terror and possibly death. Jefferson is about to discover the full meaning of that, and I can't fucking wait to watch his smug grin disappear replaced by one of desperation.

We reach my office and by the time I've taken my seat behind my desk, Jefferson is sitting in the one opposite with two of my soldiers behind him like avenging demons on his shoulder. Cesare is leaning against the wall, regarding the proceedings with his usual enigmatic look and I smile at my guest, who appears to have misplaced his swagger.

"Happy birthday, Jefferson."

He licks his lips and nods nervously. "Thank you, sir."

"Did you enjoy the party I laid on for you?"

He nods, the sweat beading on his brow as he senses he's about to pay dearly for it.

I flick on my monitor and note the blood drain from his face as he watches his starring role and the only sounds in the room are of his groans of ecstasy as he has his cake and eats it.

"What is this?" He says nervously, his tongue sliding along his dry lips as he struggles to understand what's happening.

"I thought you'd enjoy a memento of the occasion."

He says nothing and I register the sweat running down his face as he waits for the sword to fall.

I savor the moment before saying casually, "It's time to pay up."

"But I thought…"

"This was a free party?"

I shake my head as if I'm disappointed.

"You should understand that nothing is free in life, of value, anyway."

I take a moment to witness the realization settle over him and then lean forward, relishing the blood draining from his face as I say in a dark voice.

"For your information your current girlfriend sat in that chair not one hour ago and watched the same movie."

"Abigail, but…" He glances around as if she's still here, and I nod. "Yes, she was fascinated by it. Rather disgusted as it happens, and it wasn't pleasant to witness."

"What the…?" Jefferson makes to stand but is pushed

roughly back down in his seat as he says through gritted teeth, "Do you know who I am?"

Like his girlfriend, he shows a sudden spark, and it makes me snap, "I know exactly who you are. Jefferson Stevenson spoiled rich kid who lives off his father's money and reputation. A kid who had everything handed to him in life, including a bright future, the perfect fiancé, the gold-lined path to glory and a guarantee that if anything goes wrong in his life, daddy will make it all go away."

I lean back and shake my head. "However, this time I'm guessing you would rather daddy didn't learn about this particular performance. The trouble is, he may find out when his son's movie hits the internet, and his own respectable name is dragged across the tabloids. I'm guessing he will soon learn what his son does when his back is turned, when the invitations dry up to socially acceptable gatherings and his friends turn their backs on him. I'm also guessing he will be mightily pissed when he is forced to take early retirement. I mean, how can he take the moral high ground as he passes judgment on others, when his own son breaks the law at will? So, it's up to you now, Jefferson. To step up and sort your own shit out, or be the reason he loses everything he has worked his entire life for."

Jefferson turns an interesting shade of white and as he slumps in his seat, I can tell his mind is scrambling for a solution to his problem and he says wearily, "What do you want?"

"Your girlfriend."

I lean back and his head jerks up as he stares at me in astonishment. "Abigail?"

I nod. "I want to borrow her for the summer."

"But why?"

"I need her help and she has already agreed."

"To protect me." Jefferson says in surprise and for some reason, I feel like punching the arrogant little shit.

"No." I laugh slowly. "Actually, her words were, it's his shit to deal with, not mine."

I grin, loving the anger growing on Jefferson's conceited face.

"I pointed out the repercussions of this movie reaching the public domain and she agreed to save her family the embarrassment of being associated with you."

Jefferson's shoulders sag and I know I have him exactly where I want him.

"So, she becomes your..." he winces. "Girlfriend for the summer. That's it?"

I nod. "Then you can watch me burn the evidence and we all pick up where we left off with no hard feelings. You get to plan your wedding knowing your bride to be has seen your true colors and I carry on with my day. Nobody gets to witness your hobby first hand and you continue to rise like a phoenix from the ashes. Everyone's a winner. So, Jefferson, do we have a deal?"

He nods miserably. "I don't have a choice. Do I?"

"Not if you want it to all go away. No, you don't."

I stand and my men force Jefferson to his feet, and he says fearfully, "What now?"

"You leave. Wait for Abigail to break up with you and defend her decision when your parents question it. I don't care what excuse you deliver to make yourself look good. Just make sure you deflect the heat from her door. A few weeks are all I need, and then we will say no more about this unfortunate incident."

I nod to my soldiers, who pull him roughly from the room and as the door slams behind them, Cesare straightens up from his position against the wall and says darkly, "You have a problem."

CHAPTER 4

ABIGAIL

I never expected this place to be so, well, normal. I'm not sure what I thought would greet me when I walked inside, but this appears to be similar to any club I have ever been in. There are booths set against the walls and tables with chairs positioned around a dance floor. A long bar stretches the length of the room and, for the most part, people are chatting and watching a few couples on the dance floor. If anything, I'm disappointed and head to the bar to perch on a stool to try to blend in.

The bartender smiles, but it's not suggestive in any way and I wonder what the receptionist was talking about.

"What can I get you?"

"A white wine, please."

He nods. "Coming right up."

As I sit, a few men head to the bar and I'm conscious of their attention as they wait to be served. One appears to have come straight from the office and his graying hair matches the color of his suit. Another is dressed in jeans and a sweater, and he leans on the bar and glances my way with more amusement than anything else and the guy beside him openly stares and for some reason he makes my flesh creep.

He is dressed in a suit, but it's more formal. He appears to be in his late forties and his smooth-shaven jaw and well-styled hair tell me he takes care of his appearance.

He openly stares and I shift nervously on my seat, wishing I wasn't dressed like a glitter ball. The silver fringed dress that moves independently of me was perfect for the cocktail bar I met my friends in earlier. It dusts the tops of my knees, and my black sheer stockings lead down to the silver stilettos that complement the dress. My hair is long today, and the bangs sweep against my face, acting as an effective curtain against the curious stares.

The bartender serves my drink and I reach for my purse.

"Allow me."

I glance up and the more formal man has appeared by my side and places a twenty-dollar bill on the bar.

"Keep the change, Ryan." He says in a deep voice, telling me he's familiar with the staff at least, which must mean he's a regular.

His eyes fall to the band on my wrist, and he smiles suggestively.

"First time I see."

I look down. "Is that what this tells you?"

He nods. "It says approach with caution."

"Yet you did." I stare at him directly and he nods, seemingly amused.

"I was intrigued."

He shifts a little closer. "You don't look the sort to head through those doors. I'm interested in what brought you here."

I shrug. "Curiosity I suppose."

"In what way?"

My face heats as I prepare to reveal how stupid I am, and I reach for my glass and take a huge gulp.

"I suppose I like the freedom involved."

"So, you crave freedom?"

"I do." I peer up at him and he nods as if he understands, and it makes me relax a little. He doesn't seem predatory in the least, and I lower my guard a little.

"What about you? Do you come here often?" I giggle at the foolish question, and he nods. "I'm a member. It relaxes me after a hard day at the office."

"Then you must work late."

The fact it's approaching midnight, and he's still in his suit tells me that at least, and he laughs softly. "I run my own business and I don't know when to call it a night. This place is on the way home, so I indulge my guilty pleasure at least twice a week."

"Don't you have a wife and a family waiting for you?"

I'm curious, and he nods. "Both."

A shiver of excitement passes through me at his words. Despite his situation, he is still free, and I say softly, "Does your wife know you come here?"

"No." He grins wickedly and now I have the measure of him.

He leans a little closer. "This place is an addiction. Nothing escapes from inside these walls. Nobody knows what goes on and there are no repercussions. I indulge my fantasy as an escape from reality. I'm kind of guessing that's why you're here, too."

"You'd be right." My heart quickens as he smiles, the lust burning brightly in his eyes.

"Then allow me to enlighten you and show you what really happens behind closed doors."

Somehow, I knew this conversation was going to lead us here and despite the fact he's much older and not even particularly attractive, I am so keen to learn something new tonight. Images of Jefferson in that private room doing unspeakable things fired my curiosity and I've come this far, I may as well step a little closer to the flame.

"I don't have to, um, do anything, do I?"

I sound like a kid in high school as I already begin to backtrack and as his arm slides around my waist, the air is thick between us as he whispers, "We will go as far as you want to. If you decide it's not for you, then no hard feelings. I don't force myself on anyone. Just tell me to stop and I will."

My nerves settle at his words because I'm still not sure if I want this, and as I shift off the stool, I take a huge gulp of Dutch courage before following him to a door at the end of the room.

* * *

As soon as the door slams behind us, I note the atmosphere change. Silence greets us, making it appear as if we're the only ones here.

We walk down a red carpeted hallway, the black painted walls offering no clue as to what's in store, and he nods toward one of the many doors we pass.

"This one is free."

My heart almost gives out on me as he pushes it open and as I step inside, my breath catches because this is *exactly* how I pictured this place.

Red walls with restraints fixed to them burn my eyes. A large padded bench set in the middle with various devices attached makes me swallow hard. I gaze in awe at the many instruments hanging from the walls, including whips, chains and straps and drawers that I'm certain contain everything required for a night of sin.

I'm only slightly aware that he locks the door and whispers, "You can open it from the inside, but it prevents anyone from walking in on us."

He reassures me, "You can leave at any time."

I nod, mesmerized by a world I never knew was real and as I move slowly around the room, I stare in wonder at the debauchery before my eyes.

The man appears by my side and whispers, "No names are asked and no details of your life given. In here we are enigmas intent only on pleasure. No strings, no recriminations, just a night of wild enjoyment and when we walk away, nobody even knows we were here.

His lips brush against my neck and my heart starts banging as I sense I've foolishly dived headfirst into the fire, and his husky whisper startles me when he says lustfully, "Take off your dress."

Like a bucket of cold water, it brings me to my senses, and I move away and say quickly, "I'm not ready."

He steps a little closer and says, "Would it help if I turned off the lights?"

"Maybe."

My fascination with experiencing something forbidden is controlling my judgment, and he says huskily, "Then wait here. I'll be right back. I'll fetch us some champagne and then turn out the lights. Trust me to make this good for you."

I nod, still unsure how I really feel about this and as I hear the door gently close, I exhale the breath I appear to have been holding and weigh up my options.

Do I really want this?

I circle the room like a caged animal, wondering if I'm in too deep. It all seemed so delicious and exciting, but sex with that man doesn't really fulfill the fantasy I have in my mind. Do I want him to be my first? To give something so well-guarded to a stranger in a bar, old enough to be my father.

Is this what I've been waiting for? A sordid experience in a darkened sex dungeon telling me I've lost my mind as well as my principles. Then again, he could be anyone in my mind when the lights dim. I could turn over my body to a professional who knows how to play it. Not Jefferson. A man who will be forever etched in my memory, crawling across the room on his hands and knees before fucking a whore.

Do I want it to be him? A guy I thought would do, but really doesn't measure up at all. It strikes me as sad that my body is the one thing I have left to control, so it's probably now or never but am I making a huge mistake giving it to him?

So many thoughts rattle through my mind as I attempt to make a decision that will stay with me for the rest of my life. Do I want this? I want the experience, but do I want it with a complete stranger?

An image enters my mind of the man I met earlier, who I shot down in flames. My new boyfriend if he gets his way, so perhaps I should wait and experience this with him. Then again, he is just like the rest of them. A controlling bastard who took my freedom of choice away from me. Why should I give him something so treasured when he hasn't earned that right?

No, it's my decision and this could well be my only chance to make it, so with a deep gulp of air, I decide.

I'm doing this with the stranger in a suit and, for once in my life, I'm going to experience freedom.

CHAPTER 5

MATTEO

We watch Abigail enter the room with a man I want to tear apart for my own pleasure and Cesare says in a low voice, "What's the plan?"

"We give them two minutes and if they don't leave, we're going in."

My fist curls by my side as I lean against the wall, conscious of what's happening behind most of the closed doors.

The Banned Room is just another one of my clubs and when Cesare told me Abigail had come here, it shocked me. I never saw that one coming, which tells me I misread her character.

Dolly on the desk filled us in and the fact it's her first time intrigues me. Obviously, she saw something on that monitor in my office that lit a spark and if anyone is going to fan the flames, it's me.

I shift off the wall as the door opens, fully expecting them both to leave the room. However, only one person makes it out who stares in shock at the welcoming committee waiting for him.

Before he can react, he is bundled away by my men, leaving me with my trusted consigliere.

"Wait here." I hiss and he resumes his position against the wall, resigned to waiting it out.

I open the door softly and flick the switch, plunging the room into darkness.

I just make out her shimmering dress in the dusky light and can almost reach out and touch her nerves.

I say nothing and prowl toward her, stopping to grab a silk blindfold from its usual place and as I reach her, I slide her hair away from the back of her neck and trail my fingers against her skin.

She stiffens, but I don't react and carry on teasing a light path down to the base and press my lips lightly against her perfect skin, loving how she tenses at my touch.

I slip the blindfold around her eyes, noting how her breath hitches as she shivers before me and as I reach for her zipper, I waste no time in dragging it down, so her dress falls to a heap on the floor.

She makes to speak, but I press my finger lightly to her lips and her heavy breathing reveals she's intoxicated by the situation. Nervous, undoubtedly, but not attempting to stop me, and as she stands before me dressed in silk stockings and the finest lingerie, my cock twitches with an urgency it hasn't felt for some time.

Her soft breath against my lips is the sweetest sensation and I'm almost tempted to dip in for a taste. However, she obviously craves the experience, so I drop to my knees instead and pull down her panties, her shocked gasp making me smile.

I part her thighs and nuzzle against the sweet scent of a girl aching to become a woman and, as I flick my tongue against her clit, her low moan matches the wet heat encouraging me on.

There is no noise in the room except for her heavy, gasping breath and as I coax and tease her sodden clit, her gasp of pleasure makes me smile.

Who knew she would turn out to be such a naughty girl?

As I pull away, I press two fingers inside, causing her to gasp out loud and the resistance I find tells me this is her first time. Another surprise and not an unwelcome one. Just how I like them. Fresh for the picking.

I push in deeper, and she gasps as she tenses, and I push her back until she hits the edge of the padded bench. Turning her around, I press her forward until she is face down with her ass pointing high in my direction.

Reaching across, I slip her wrist into one of the restraints, causing her to panic a little and so I lean down and whisper, "Trust me."

She tenses as my face catches hers and yet allows me to secure her other wrist, so she is fully restrained.

Then I reach for the soft fur glove that rests on the shelf below and as I run it across her ass, she shivers at the decadent touch. Her gentle moan tells me she's heavy with lust and removing the fur glove, I slap my palm against her ass – hard.

"Fuck!" she calls out and as I press light kisses on the sting, she groans out loud as I rub the burn and reach for her hair.

Fisting it in my hand, I pull her head back and whisper, "What do you want?"

She answers with a tortured gasp. "You."

The next sound is my zipper as I release my impatient cock and as I press it against her ass, she moans out loud.

"Do you want me to fuck you, princess?"

For a second she tenses, and I almost think she'll back out, but her agonized voice hits me once again with surprise.

"Yes. Do it."

I sheath my cock and press against her from behind, my fingers massaging her clit until she groans into the bench. She is so wet, so eager and so willing and I whisper huskily, "Last chance, princess."

"Please. Take it."

I still for a second because this is interesting. She obviously wants to rid herself of something that she was preserving for her marital bed. Then I'm shocked when a rare spark of emotion hits me hard, as it all becomes clear what this is.

She obviously senses my hesitation because she growls, "Do it. I'm begging you."

There is something so sad about her request, but I understand it. I understand *her*, so without another word, I push in hard and fast, her agonized scream bouncing off the padded walls as I rip through her innocence.

"Oh my God." She sobs into the padded bench as she experiences the burn and I massage her clit and press light kisses on the back of her neck as I move slower, more carefully, allowing her body to adjust to the invasion.

Now the initial pain has gone, she relaxes and I sense the heat building between us. The sweat runs down her back as she becomes accustomed to me inside and as I ride her, I try to make it pleasurable. I am tender, patient and focused on her needs entirely and as she cries out, the orgasm rips through her body at lightning speed. Her walls throb and her legs shake, and her tortured cry causes me to come so hard it surprises me. I can't remember the last time it was so intense and that shocks me a little.

As she crashes back to reality, she slumps onto the bench, sobbing into the red leather as I pull out, discarding the condom and zipping up my pants, conscious of the broken woman splayed out in front of me.

I untie her wrists gently and, keeping the blindfold on, I leave her crying for her stolen virginity and depart the room as silently as I came.

Cesare shifts off the wall and throws me a quizzical glance and I growl, "Make sure she gets home safely."

He nods and as I walk from the club, it's with a rare smile on my face as I contemplate a very interesting summer ahead.

CHAPTER 6

ABIGAIL

I don't know why I'm crying. It's as if the dam has burst and I can't control the river. It hurt so much, but what came next was exhilarating. I never expected that and as my pussy throbs and my ass stings, I feel the mess between my legs, knowing there is no going back.

I did it. I'm a woman now and *I* made it happen.

I stand tentatively and slip to the floor where my dress lies discarded with my panties. The room is still in darkness, which is fine by me.

What just happened?

For a moment I sit, trying to process everything that just occurred, and then a smile stretches across my face as I shiver inside.

He was here.

The moment he entered the room, I realized he wasn't the previous man. God knows how, but his scent wafted toward me almost immediately. Fancy aftershave mixed with alcohol and cigars. The same smell that lingered in his office that intoxicated me almost as much as his presence.

His husky voice registered in my subconscious and when

his face brushed against my skin, it was rough, not smooth like the man before him.

I could tell it was that bastard without even seeing him and I had an overwhelming urge for him to be the one I flung my virginity at like a discarded rag I couldn't wait to see the back of.

I'm glad it was him.

I *wanted* it to be him, and it *was* him.

I know it.

The fact he's left is a blessing because I'm not sure I could face him after what we just did.

As I dress slowly, I bring my breathing under control and think about how to play this. He wants me to rebel, to go against my parents and become his girlfriend.

How the fuck do I go about that?

He obviously doesn't realize how guarded my life is, and then there's Jefferson. How do I broach the subject with him without revealing everything I know?

Despite every problem battling for answers, there is an overwhelming feeling inside me that rises above all the others.

I did it.

I'm a woman now. *His* woman and nothing can ever take that away from me. I made my own decision, and it worked out for once. He will forever hold the honor of being my first and whatever happens next, nothing can change that.

* * *

Somehow, I make it to the door and resist switching on the light to stare at a scene that is best left in the dark. Nothing to see here, just an incredible memory that will be mine to treasure whatever happens next.

As I pass through the hallway, I picture what's happening

behind every darkened door and wonder if I'll ever be back. Will I discover all the secrets these rooms hold? If I'm married to Jefferson, I'll sign up for membership on my way out. Like the man I met, it could become my guilty secret, no questions asked.

For some reason, that makes me smile and as I walk through the bar with my head held high, I act as if I belong here.

"Hey, how did it go?" The receptionist peers at me with curiosity and I smile.

"Amazing. Thank you."

She seems surprised. "Did you…?"

"Yes." I laugh softly. "I may even be back."

"Wow!" She shakes her head. "I've gotta hand it to you. You've got balls."

"Thanks for giving me the chance."

She nods. "Anytime, sister."

"I don't suppose you could call me a cab?" I ask, knowing I really should be getting home by now.

"There's one waiting outside. It's all yours." She winks and as I make to leave, I turn back and say quickly, "I'd say goodbye, but I have a feeling I'll be back."

"I've no doubt, honey."

She laughs out loud. "It's the thrill you see. The forbidden. We can all lose ourselves and leave real life outside the door. It's intoxicating and better than any drug."

"You've got that right."

I turn away and head outside, noting the black car waiting with a man standing by the open door.

"Where to?" He says gruffly, and I stare at him in surprise.

"You don't seem like a cab."

He shrugs. "It's the only way you're getting home tonight, so you may as well get in."

A shiver runs down my spine as the penny drops and as I

slide into the darkened interior, my thoughts turn to the man whose car this is.

Matteo Ortega.

What on earth am I going to do about him? Seriously sexy, completely domineering and so forbidden, my panties are soaked already.

My boyfriend and whatever his reason is, I'm going to play this to my advantage.

The door slams behind me and the man jumps into the passenger seat and as the car pulls away from the club, I smile into the darkness.

Yes, Matteo Ortega may think he holds all the cards the domineering bastard, but he hasn't met me yet, not really and what happened back there will never be mentioned, not by me, anyway and it will be interesting to see how long he can keep it a secret.

* * *

I WAKE the next morning with a dull ache between my legs and a satisfied smile on my face. I still can't comprehend what happened last night. My safe ordered life was set on fire the moment I saw Jefferson on all fours, and I walked away and struck a match under my own one. My only regret is that I didn't do it sooner and my thoughts immediately turn to the man who made it all happen.

Matteo Ortega is dangerous. A bad boy of the most volatile kind. Lock up your daughters the devil's in town and for some reason our paths have crossed, and he has me in his sights.

My phone vibrates and I note the many texts lighting it up and I grab it fast. There are several from Jefferson, Clarice and only one from an unknown number.

I open that one first.

> **WITHELD NUMBER**
>
> Be ready at 2 pm

Shit! This is happening.

I actually feel sick now because shit just got real. My parents are going to blow their stack.

I turn to Jefferson's and it's obvious he knows.

> **JEFFERSON**
>
> Honey, call me. I can explain.

> **JEFFERSON**
>
> Don't be mad at me. I'll cover for you if you cover for me.

> **JEFFERSON**
>
> We can get through this if we stick together.

> **JEFFERSON**
>
> I'll back you up. Just tell your parents we're taking a break for a few weeks to make sure this is what we both want. Tell them I'm giving you some space to enjoy the single life before committing your future to me.

> **JEFFERSON**
>
> Call me honey. I'm going out of my mind here.

With a sigh, I scroll through the ones from my best friend.

> **CLARICE**
>
> Hey, babe. You missed a great night. Oscar Mahoney was in town, and guess where I woke up? Call me for the juicy details.

> **CLARICE**
>
> Are you still sleeping? Man, that migraine must have sucked.

> **CLARICE**
>
> Make sure you're at brunch today. I've got so much to tell you.

I laugh to myself when I picture the expression on her face if I told her what happened regarding my night. She wouldn't believe it because Abigail Kensington is the model child.

If anything, I am invigorated and have never felt so alive. I'm a woman now and make my own choices and if Jefferson thinks I'm ever going to take his shit, he's got another thing coming.

Somehow, I haul my ass into the shower and cleanse away my sins under the hot steamy water and soap them away with the finest products. I should feel dirty. I should be scrubbing my shame away, but instead I'm basking in it. I love the new me. The confident woman who takes no shit. Not anymore because I've learned I have choices, and it's up to me to make them count.

I change into my usual Sunday best. A smart dress for church that will be acceptable for brunch. I normally accompany my parents to Seagrasses, where we meet up with Jefferson and his family. Clarice is usually there with her family, so it will be an interesting one today.

As I head downstairs, I leave all my texts unanswered. What would I say anyway?

My parents are waiting impatiently by the door and my mother casts a critical eye over my appearance before nodding. "I suppose you will have to do. Come, we're five minutes late already. Shape up Abigail, tardiness is not an attractive quality."

Even my mother can't dull my shine today and I catch my father's eye as I walk past. He appears thoughtful and as my mother sweeps through the front door, his hand on my arm holds me back and he says in a low voice, "Just so you know, I'm not happy about this."

"What?" I'm confused, wondering if somehow he can read minds and he sighs.

"Jefferson."

"What about him?" Now I'm nervous and he exhales sharply. "He's not good enough for you. He never was."

"I don't understand." I really don't because as far as I know, my father gave his blessing for our arrangement.

There is something bothering my father. It's obvious, and he says with a sigh. "I wish things were different, that's all."

He nods toward the door, reminding me my mother is waiting and as we exit into the sunshine, I'm left with even more questions. We take up our usual positions in the car and as I settle into my role as the dutiful daughter, something is telling me that today, everything will change.

CHAPTER 7

MATTEO

I sit on my terrace at the table set for breakfast. The view of my garden is immeasurable. A stone terrace with steps leading down onto a manicured grass area. Through an arch at the end, a formal garden journeys down to a glittering lake. I have everything money can buy, but I am the poorest man I know because I'm alone. That I've always been alone is the saddest fact of all.

When I fell out with my family over a woman, I vowed never to love again. She destroyed us all. Diana came into our lives and tore it apart from the inside. She seduced three brothers and then married their father, who in turn sent us away. I have an uneasy truce with my brothers now, but my sister wasn't so lucky.

Eliza was left behind and something happened to make her run, resulting in my father hunting her down with a view to bringing her home.

They never made it. They were both blown to pieces on a yacht in Dubai, leaving my stepmother firmly in charge. She had already moved her brother Mario in, and they now sit at the head of the family, intent on only one thing. Taking control and driving us out.

That's why I need Abigail. She doesn't know it yet, but Mario has it bad for her. Apparently, she's the one woman he wanted but never had, and my plan is to wave my new toy in his face to drive a reaction.

It hurts that Diana is in love with him. The fact he's not really her brother makes a mockery of my father all over again. He trusted her and welcomed Mario into his home, not knowing his new wife was screwing him when his back was turned. Mario and Diana are the worst kind of humans and with my brother's help, their lives are about to be cut short.

Cesare approaches and I wave my hand to the chair beside me.

"That was some night." He says with a sly grin, and I adjust my dark shades against the sun.

"It was interesting."

"So, what's the plan today?"

He pours an orange juice from the jug and regards me with interest,

"Brunch."

He raises his eyes, probably because the last thing we ever do is brunch. Not to mention the piles of food set on this table before us makes it a pointless exercise.

"Will you be traveling light?"

"There is no need for protection. We will be dining with Jared Kensington and his family."

Cesare laughs softly. "Does his daughter know?"

"I doubt it."

He shakes his head. "How did you make that happen?"

The fact I'm known to be from the wrong side of town won't help Jared's image, but he owes me a favor and I'm calling it in.

"I contacted him this morning and made him an offer he couldn't refuse."

"Which is?" Cesare is hungry for information, which is why we get along. Like me, he thrives on moving the chess pieces around the board with only one aim in mind. The win.

"It appears that Jared Kensington isn't as respectable as he likes people to believe. He has a nasty habit that has come to my attention."

"Interesting." Cesare's eyes are lit with interest, and I grin.

"I discovered he invested heavily in a company called Optimum a few years back. It's an engineering business that, on the outside, is very respectable and makes a good profit every year."

"I don't believe I've heard of it."

"You wouldn't. It has no interest for us except when you study the fine print. Optimum is part of a group of companies and far down the list, hidden in the small print, is a company called Android."

Cesare sits up and his eyes burn with delight.

"Now that is interesting."

I nod. "Yes. The good billionaire is funding arms to hostile territories, and if it became public knowledge, he would be ostracized and his credibility in tatters. It could burn his whole fucking life down, which is why a seat at his brunch table is a small price to pay for my silence."

"Checkmate, Matteo."

Cesare raises his glass to mine, and we take a moment to enjoy the sun on our faces and the sweet breath of fresh air that blows away the shit that surrounds us.

"What happens after brunch?"

Cesare interrupts the silence and I stretch out and sigh.

"We bring our guest home."

"Miss. Kensington, I presume."

"Of course. Tell Baines to instruct the staff. Our visitor will require the guest suite."

Cesare rolls his eyes, causing me to grin wickedly.

"One step at a time, Cesare. Allow the cat to play with his food before he eats."

My phone vibrates and I note my brother on the other end and snap,

"Leo. How can I help you?"

"Just checking in. What's your position regarding the girl?"

"I'm moving her in today."

"Good. Dom and Flora are all set. We need you to wrap this one up."

"Consider it done already."

I'm curious and say quickly, "Have you read the will yet?"

Leonardo's part in our plan is to get eyes on our father's will before we head to the reading next week. Knowing my father, there is a nasty surprise waiting for us, and it's imperative we discover what it is so we can deal with it before the event.

"I should have eyes on it later on tonight."

Leonardo is my older brother. Domenico is younger than me and even though we were set against one another, we have somehow come together to defeat our stepmother, Diana. Domenico used her sister to steal the money that Diana stole from our father and the funds are now in place to run the Ortega empire. Diana is pissed and wants her money back, but Dom has hidden it away so she can never find it. My mission is to bring Mario down and Abigail is the perfect weapon for that.

"Keep us informed."

I say with a sigh and Leo says snappily, *"I can't wait to see those fuckers burn."*

"Me too brother."

I cut the call because even though we put our rift behind us, we're still not at the stage where we make polite conversation. I have Cesare for that, so I push back my seat and say firmly, "We should get this day started. The devil dances on the sabbath while the innocent rest."

Cesare laughs out loud and follows me into the house.

CHAPTER 8

ABIGAIL

Church was the usual photo opportunity. The place to be seen for any respectable family keeping up appearances. The fact Jefferson was sitting in the pew behind, as usual, was inconvenient and I managed to ignore him for the best part of the service by staring straight ahead and pretending to be engrossed in my hymn book.

We didn't hang around afterward and are now making our way to Seagrasses for the next hurdle to jump.

Brunch.

"You were quite rude to Jefferson back there."

Mom snaps as soon as we take our seats in the car.

"I don't know what you mean." I say it politely, but her eyes narrow.

"Have you fallen out?"

"Yes."

I don't try to dress it up because it may make it easier when I break her heart later today.

"Then fix it."

"Excuse me." I blink in surprise because she hasn't even

asked why. Apparently, nothing can be bad enough to steer me away from the path she has set me on.

"You heard me, Abigail. Whatever Jefferson has done to annoy you is inconsequential. We have an agenda to adhere to and unity in our families must be preserved."

"Why?" She wasn't expecting me to answer back, and she stares at me with disdain.

"Because you are to be married regardless of any indiscretion that may have occurred."

"I never mentioned an indiscretion."

I stare at her through narrowed eyes because obviously mom knows more than she's letting on.

"Don't narrow your eyes at me, Abigail. You will not disrespect me."

She throws me a withering glare and then sighs.

"Mary called this morning before we left. Apparently, Jefferson told her that he was a little wild last night and you found out and were angry. He was concerned and decided to give you some space while you simmered down. He is such a gentleman. You don't find many like him, Abigail, so congratulate yourself on finding a respectable man."

I stare at her in shock and as I catch my father's eye, he shakes his head.

"What else did Mary say, Anna?"

I'm not sure who is more surprised that he spoke, me or my mother, because daddy always keeps out of domestic issues as he calls it.

She recovers well and says sharply, "That Jefferson is worried he has ruined things. He will do anything to make it better."

"What did he do?"

My father's voice is sharp and offers no room for argument and mom falters before saying with a dismissive wave of her hand, "He had too much to drink in the Ortega club last night. He was a little inappropriate with the staff and fears photographic evidence coming out. Apparently, someone at the club informed Abigail and now he's afraid she will not agree to the engagement."

My father stares at me and I register the anger in his eyes as he says slowly, "Inappropriate. I see."

I hold my breath as he directs his next question to me.

"Who sent you the evidence?"

I don't know what to say and shrug. "It was anonymous."

I hate lying to my father, but if I tell him who really sent it, he will never allow me to date the guy. At least that's the story we're going with, although that seems like a far-fetched scenario right now.

"Show me." He holds out his hand for my phone and I say quickly, "I deleted it."

My mother nods her approval. "Thank goodness for that. Finally, you demonstrate common sense. No, it's best to forget all about the unfortunate incident and now you need to make it evident that you forgive Jefferson at brunch."

My father sits back in his seat looking thoughtful and as the car pulls up outside Seagrasses, I'm grateful for the opportunity to escape this conversation.

We head inside and I cringe when we are shown to our usual table and Jefferson is waiting for me, my chair pulled back beside him.

It's almost as if he's got guilty tattooed on his face as he whispers, "I'm sorry, honey."

I ignore him and smile at his mother and father politely.

Mary peers at me with concern and I can tell they are anxious because this marriage benefits both families and any scandal attached would impact everyone around this table.

I'm surprised to note two empty seats on either side of my

father and the Judge obviously notices them too because he says with interest, "Are we expecting anyone else?"

Before my father can speak, I hear the husky voice from my nightmares.

"Good morning, Mr. Kensington. Mrs. Kensington."

I freeze along with Jefferson beside me as the voice addresses his parents. "Judge Stevenson, it's been a long time, and this must be your lovely wife, Mary."

I almost can't look, but as my head turns, I meet the dark, dangerous eyes of the man I desire more than my sanity and hate with a passion.

"Miss. Kensington." He smiles and I hate the flutter that passes through my body like a Mexican wave.

I say nothing and look away as Matteo Ortega takes the seat beside my father on one side, and his friend on the other.

That man is no different and wears danger like a fucking badge of pride. They have brought intensity to our table and any light atmosphere has been chased away by the darkness. I'm interested to watch my mother's reaction and her tightly pursed lips indicate she is not at all happy, which gives me a moment's pleasure. I'm pretty sure Jefferson is shitting himself right now and the sharp look his father directs at him tells me he hasn't got a clue what's going on either.

As brunch gets underway, I'm conscious of Matteo's eyes locked on me the entire time. Just him being here is making it difficult to breathe and not because of the fear of what he may do. It's him. The prince of darkness, crouching and ready to pounce. I can almost taste it. Reach out and touch it because whatever his game is, it's one he intends on winning.

My father does his best to keep the conversation light, but I note the weariness in his eyes as he struggles to hold it together. Mom is unnaturally quiet and Mary, opposite me, is nervous. Jefferson is mute and keeps checking his phone as if the answer lies there somehow, and then my heart jumps when Matteo says in his dark voice.

"Miss. Kensington."

I look up, nervous to meet his eyes and the amusement in them irritates me, so I say casually, "Mr. Ortega."

"I have a business proposition for you."

The tension at the table is at breaking point as my mom gasps and stares at my father in the vain hope he will put a stop to whatever this is.

"I'm not in business, Mr. Ortega."

My voice is calm and controlled and even when his eyes flash, I don't let it affect me.

He leans forward and stares at me hard. "I am in need of an escort for the summer."

My mom's harsh intake of breath is almost enjoyable as he grins. "An assistant if you like. Somebody of impeccable breeding and decency. A morally incorrupt young woman who can accompany me to my father's funeral."

Mom is trying so hard to hold it together as Matteo looks slyly at my father. "Your father has agreed to the appointment. Four weeks work for a generous donation to his preferred charity. Charity work if you like, the perfect way to spend the summer."

I regard him coolly and then peer at my father for his reaction and the defeat in his eyes tells me there is more to this than I thought. Obviously, my father is hiding something that Matteo Ortega is holding over him and the threat may as well be sitting at the center of the table for everyone to see.

I continue to stare into Matteo's eyes and realize this has been done to remove me from my current situation. He set me up and I have no choice. Jefferson is rigid beside me but nudges me under the table with his leg and I couldn't hate him any more than I do because it's obvious he's intent on saving his own reputation at the cost of mine.

Every single pair of eyes around the table, if not the restaurant, are trained on us as I nod coolly. "How can I turn down money for charity?"

Mom makes to speak, but the fierce glare from my father has her backing down in an instant and Matteo sits back in his chair and nods.

"Then it is agreed. Abigail leaves with me and will return in four weeks' time, no doubt to an engagement party and an amazing life with the fine young man beside her."

I steal a glance at my father, who returns it with an almost apologetic glint in his eye and I smile reassuringly. Whatever Matteo has on my father, I'm going to make sure it's never used against him. I love my father even though he isn't around much and leaves everything to mom, but I know he always has my best interests at heart.

I'm a little shocked when Matteo stands, along with his companion and nods in my direction.

"We are leaving. Ladies, gentlemen, it's been a pleasure."

He heads my way and as I stand, he pulls back my chair and I swear every eye in Seagrasses is trained on this scene, and I know it will be the gossip of the season.

His fingers brush against my arm as he walks by my side out of the restaurant and only the horrified stare of my best friend seated nearby tells me my life is screwed before it even begun.

CHAPTER 9

MATTEO

It's good to be me, most of the time, anyway. I just walked into that restaurant and set six lives on fire and it's not even lunchtime yet. It gives me a natural high and I'm in a great mood as I guide my prize through the aghast faces surrounding us as we leave respectability behind for a world of sin and depravation.

Abigail is straight-backed and controlled beside me and is perfect. Beautiful, elegant and poised with a calm, controlled manner that will serve her well. As I cast my mind back on the sobbing woman who came apart under me last night, you would never think it was the same person. I will enjoy wrecking the cool façade she hides behind because I have a feeling Abigail Kensington is guarding a center of molten fire.

We reach my car that is parked outside the entrance and one of my soldiers holds the door open. Cesare steps into the car in front, allowing me time with my guest on the short drive.

As the door slams, she says icily, "I see timekeeping is not your speciality."

I say nothing and she hisses. "2 pm. What changed?"

"On the contrary, Miss. Kensington." I lean back in my seat and rest my arm along the back of it, my fingers barely touching the back of her neck, and I smile. "My timing is impeccable. I just never mentioned what's happening at 2 pm."

She edges further away and says with disdain.

"Then enlighten me."

I glance down at her shapely legs, dressed in pantyhose with her ankles crossed above her sharp nude stilettos. Her beige shift dress is the epitome of elegance, and her freshly washed hair is carefully pulled into a chignon behind her. Abigail Kensington is American royalty, and it's no wonder her marriage has been arranged. That makes this even more delicious, and I shrug, appearing unconcerned.

"All in good time."

We make the rest of the journey in silence and I've no doubt she is wondering what's going on. She should be afraid, very afraid, because what I have planned for this woman is nothing short of evil.

Rather than head home, we come to a stop at the airfield, and she says quickly, 'What's happening?"

The door opens and as I step out, I reach for her hand. "We're taking a trip, princess."

She remains in her seat.

"Where?" Her eyes flash as she asks her question and I almost groan out loud. No wonder Mario is besotted with this woman. I'm definitely seeing the attraction because that bastard gets off on control and the woman staring coolly at me would challenge even the most dominant male.

Rather than answer her, I decide to show her who she's dealing with and removing my gun, I aim it at her head, loving the blood draining from her face as her eyes widen in fear.

"Get out of the car, princess and speak when you're spoken to."

This has the desired effect, and she is soon scrambling from the car, all her earlier bravado left in tatters on the floor.

Grabbing her arm, I manhandle her up the steps into the plane and note the amused glances of my flight crew who have seen this all before.

Pushing her into a seat, I snarl, "Now buckle up, baby, and enjoy the ride."

She doesn't even question me and I'm a little disappointed about that.

As I take my seat opposite her, the flight attendant offers me a whiskey and a flute of champagne for my guest.

It amuses me when she accepts it with shaking fingers and drains the glass entirely before leaning back and closing her eyes, effectively shutting me out.

Cesare shakes his head and grins as he takes his seat beside her and opposite me and as the plane taxis to the runway, I wonder what she'll make of our destination.

It doesn't take long before we're airborne, and she surprises me by opening her eyes and fixing me with a cool expression.

"Where are we going?"

I bite back my irritation because for fuck's sake, doesn't she understand basic instruction now?

Before I can shoot her down and remind her what I said back there, she shrugs. "I only ask because that was too easy."

"What was?" Cesare looks up and she shrugs.

"The restaurant. You must have something on my father for him to allow this to happen—whatever this is."

She waves her hand around the plane, and I catch Cesare's eye, who is suddenly more alert.

"Perhaps daddy doesn't want his investments becoming common knowledge."

"His investments?"

"Arms mainly."

She appears more interested than shocked and shakes her

head. "So what? He has enough lawyers to deflect any heat from him. I'm almost positive that wasn't the reason."

Now she has my full attention and I say with interest.

"Does it matter?"

"Not to me, but I'd be questioning everything if I were you."

"What makes you say that?"

I'm starting to get irritated, and she leans forward and stares me straight in the eye.

"All of my life, I've been controlled by my parents. What to do, say, and how to act. They have molded me into the person I am today, and it was for one thing. Marriage to the best."

"And you think that's Jefferson?"

I laugh out loud, and she shrugs. "I never questioned it, but something my father said made me doubt that."

"What did he say?"

"That Jefferson wasn't good enough for me and he wished things were different."

"So, he took the first exit he could and pushed you through it?"

I'm a little surprised by this conversation because I never considered for one minute that Jared had his own agenda. I believed I was the one calling the shots, but now I'm not so sure.

She leans back and says coolly, "I'll ask you again, where are we going?"

"And I'll tell you again, you'll know when I damn well want you to."

I stand and motion for Cesare to follow me and as we reach the back of the plane, I snap at the attendant.

"Bring the bottle of whiskey and two glasses."

Cesare grins with amusement as I rake my fingers through my hair and take the seat by the window.

"She makes a valid point." Cesare says as he sits opposite

and takes the glass from the attendant, who can't move quickly enough.

As he pours the whiskey into our glasses before he leaves, I replay what Abigail said. Something is telling me she's right and I say to my friend, "What are your thoughts?"

"That there's more to this than we gave Jared credit for. It struck me as odd that he agreed to the meeting in full view of Washington's elite. To allow his daughter to leave with us was social suicide."

"Or he wanted someone to know."

"Do you think we were set up?"

"Possibly." I swirl the liquid around my glass and cast my mind back on the people at the table.

"Do you believe Judge Stevenson was in on it?"

"He was mighty quiet the entire time."

"They all were."

Cesare exhales sharply. "I'll do some digging. Maybe you should be a bit nicer to our guest. She may have something to give us."

"You think?" I let his words register for a while as I digest them. Perhaps she does have information that could help and she's right there was a reason her father played along without a fight.

"Does it change your plans?"

Cesare interrupts my thoughts and I shake my head.

"No. If anything, it makes it even more important because if they are playing games and setting us up, I'm taking his daughter down with me."

CHAPTER 10

ABIGAIL

I've thought of nothing else since we left the restaurant. Something doesn't feel right. It was too easy and knowing my parents, I never expected them to give me up without a fight. When I asked what Matteo had on my father, I believed it would make everything clear, but an investment, that's just not enough. Daddy has invested in dubious companies before, and his lawyers eat any challenges for breakfast. Unless he's murdered anyone, nothing can touch him, so whatever it is must concern me somehow.

My head aches with it all and I'm surprised when Matteo heads back without his usual shadow and sits beside me and then leans closer and whispers, "The answer to your question is Vegas."

"Why there?"

"So we can get married."

I stare at him in shock and note the dark intent in his eyes and I hiss, "I don't understand."

He trails his fingers against my neck, and I forget to breathe as he closes his hand around my throat and increases the pressure slightly.

"Because that is the best way to protect my investment."

His hand moves and twists my face to his and my eyes water as the pain grips me hard. The anger in those eyes causes me to catch my breath as he allows me to step inside his black soul for the briefest second.

"You will do whatever the fuck I tell you, because your destiny is in my hands. If you want to make it back to your safe life and gold-lined future with the fool you left behind, you won't question me. You will do whatever I say because it's of no consequence to me whether you make it back at all."

My eyes fill with tears as he leans closer and whispers against my lips, "So in your own interest, it may be advisable to tell me what you know, and I'll be the judge of whether it's important enough."

I gasp as he tightens his grip and his low husky voice wafts through my entire body, like toxic black smoke.

"Last night was only the beginning, princess. Did you like it? Did you like my cock inside you, ripping away your innocence? Are you imagining how good it will be to be controlled and dominated by me? Allow me to make your decisions for you. Give you more pleasure than you believed possible and expect total obedience in return."

He pulls me even closer and whispers, "You see, disobey me and you won't like the punishment. The moment you stepped foot inside the Banned Room, your fate was sealed. I now own every part of you inside and out and you only get to leave when I fucking say so."

He releases his hold, and my hands fly to my neck as I struggle to breathe, certain there must be a bruise forming already.

Then he says dismissively, "You have no choice. Marry me at 2 pm today and forget you ever had a mind of your own."

He stands and walks away, leaving me fucking terrified.

I can't believe the mess I'm in. Why did I ever want that

man? He's vile. Rough, crude and disgusting. Then why do I suddenly wish I had a change of underwear because that turned me on way more than I care to admit?

I turn my face to the window and take a few deep breaths because God have mercy on my soul. I just made a deal with the devil, and it's scripted in my bloodied virginity.

* * *

I DON'T SEE him for the rest of the flight and as soon as we land, his friend, for want of a better word, stops by my seat and says firmly, "Come."

I don't even ask where his bastard boss is and just unfasten my seatbelt and follow him to the door. He stands back and points to the third black car waiting on the tarmac.

"Your ride awaits."

I don't even see Matteo, but I can feel him. It's as if his eyes are burning into me and branding me as his. I'm almost positive he's sitting behind one of the blackened windows, watching my humiliation as I try to walk with my head held high.

The door is open, and I slide inside the car, the door slamming behind me, leaving me alone.

My fingers shake as I reach inside my purse for my phone because as God is my witness, I need to get help, and fast.

It's not there.

I rummage inside, but the fact it's empty tells me the bastard stole it. Now I have nothing but a Chanel lipstick and the clothes I'm wearing to my name.

As the car heads off, following the two in front, I picture that bastard chatting with his friend. How dare he almost kidnap me and force me into marriage? What's he playing at? He knows I'm about to be engaged to Jefferson.

As we speed through Vegas, I try to get my breathing under

control. I'm panicking and that's never a good thing. Surely my parents don't know this is happening. If anything, it would finish my mother off watching her daughter marry into the mafia. It's obvious what he is, what they are, and now I will be too. From billionaire princess to mafia bride all in a morning.

We reach a chapel, and my nerves threaten to explode and end my life because I half hoped he was kidding. The fact I only half hoped it shows me what a nut job I am because there is still half of me that can't wait. Why can't I wait to be chained to a pig? A controlling, dominant, seriously sexy and devilishly handsome dark prince. Yes, that's the formula every fairy tale uses—for the fucking bad guy!

Since when did Cinderella marry the bad guy? This is one twisted fairy tale I'm living and it's obvious I'm going slightly mad even comparing it to that.

I'm having a full-blown panic attack when the door opens and his friend holds out his hand and says darkly, "Your cooperation would be appreciated."

He shifts, so his jacket falls open revealing his gun, telling me this is one shotgun wedding that is everything it says on the tin.

As I step outside, I notice a woman standing nearby, holding a bundle of fabric. As I straighten up, she steps forward and smiles. "Arms up, honey."

"What?"

"Now." The dark assassin beside me growls and, in a frantic moment of surrender, I reach for the heavens, allowing her to slip a full-blown wedding dress over my head.

As the fabric falls, she thrusts a bouquet into my trembling hands and steps back, peering with curiosity at the circus unfolding before her eyes.

I watch as she beckons another girl forward, who hands her a bouquet, and they step behind me as the strangest bridesmaids.

"Relax." Matteo's assistant says almost kindly and takes my arm in his as he guides me through the church door.

The music starts to play and as we move down the aisle, I almost want to giggle at the spectacle inside as I witness the hordes of men in black, squashed into seats on either side of the aisle.

As I reach the bastard waiting for me, I purposefully don't look at him and stare straight ahead at the 'priest' who could be just about anyone.

As he begins to recite the marriage vows, I am conscious of the man beside me, and I swear I couldn't hate anyone more than I do him right now.

"Repeat after me…"

We say our vows after the priest and my voice resembles a ball of tightly controlled fury, telling everyone present I am not happy about this.

As Matteo slips a ring on my finger, I am momentarily stunned at the sheer size of the diamond glistening before my eyes. A simple gold band accompanies it and as I ram a matching one down on his finger hard, hoping it hurts like crazy, I hear the words I've been dreading.

"I now pronounce you husband and wife. You may now kiss your bride."

A strong hand snakes around my waist and before I can react, his fingers grasp my chin and force my lips to his. As his tongue reaches inside and dominates mine, I am conscious of only one thing. The desire running like a river of betrayal between my legs because, despite my hatred, this man turns my light on every fucking time.

CHAPTER 11

MATTEO

I love it when a plan comes together and now Abigail's my wife, there is nothing Mario can do about it. He'll have to kill me first, which I'm positive is his intention, anyway.

When I saw Abigail walking down the aisle, refusing to even acknowledge me, it made me hard.

She is the most beautiful woman I have ever met and certainly out of my league. There is such a high wall she crouches behind, and yet last night I saw what's hiding there. She is passionate and strong and capable of more than she gives herself credit for and now it will be my pleasure to educate her in what that involves.

So, I kiss her with a hunger that's been building since last night because ever since I sampled perfection, I am determined to make it mine.

My plans for my wife include total domination and for my plan to work when we meet Mario, she needs to be devoted to me. So, I'm keen to begin her lessons on that and as I tear myself away, I love the lust-filled eyes and slightly crazed look on her face as she gasps for air.

"Congratulations, boss."

"Thank you, Cesare."

I nod to my men who all stand and clap loudly and I can't prevent the shit-eating grin spreading across my face.

We leave the church and step into the middle car, and as soon as the door closes, my bride surprises me with a gift of her own and punches me squarely in the face.

"What was that for?"

I shake my head as she says furiously, "For everything."

"You weren't complaining last night." I smirk and she raises her arm, which I catch in an iron fist.

Then I pull her over my knee and lift her dress, delivering sharp blows onto her peachy fine ass.

Her screams turn me on, so I carry on until she sobs, "Please, enough."

I regard her smarting ass with pride before carefully replacing the dress and pushing her back in her seat.

"Never do that again." I hiss and she sobs. "Same."

"Are you sure about that? It can be a turn on."

"For a sick bastard." She gulps and I shake my head. "You'll learn, and I'll take great pleasure in teaching you how pleasurable pain can be."

"What, like being married to a controlling bastard? Will you teach me how much fun that can be?"

She fires back and I reach out, loving how she flinches away from me and grabbing her hair, I pull her face to mine.

"Remember, I control you princess and unless you do everything I say, this won't be pleasant for you. If you cooperate, I will make it a pleasure. It's your choice."

It's as if all the fight goes out of her as she sags against me and as I tilt her face to mine, I whisper against her lips, "I will break you, princess and you'll love every fucking minute of it."

She blinks and a few tears fall from her eyes that I lick away with a groan. Then I touch her lips lightly with mine and kiss her slowly and leisurely, intent on giving her pleasure rather than pain.

She weakens in my arms and as I deepen the kiss, she begins to respond, allowing me to hold her face gently in my hands as I taste my wife for the second time already.

Her low moan tells me she's loving the softer approach, and as she shifts closer, I curl my hand around the back of her head and hold it firmly in place.

I run my hand up underneath her skirt and feel the soft skin beneath my touch and inch my fingers inside her soaked panties, loving how ready she is. As I insert two fingers inside her, she groans, and I push in deeper, searching for the sweetest spot.

I kiss her constantly, enjoying every minute of it and her thumping heart is throbbing against my chest as she stiffens before coming all over my fingers.

I remove them and insert them into her mouth so she can clean them off and as she sucks them, she stares deep into my eyes.

The car stops, interrupting the sweetest moment, and she hastily shifts off me and stares the other way, leaving me with a broad grin on my face. My little princess just can't help herself. She says one thing and totally means another. She's perfect.

We don't hang around in Vegas. My brother Dom lives here and is currently entertaining Diana's sister Flora, and I can't take the chance that Abigail will make the connection. I want to note her reaction when she sees Mario again and more than anything, I'm anticipating his. What will he do when the love of his life walks in married to me? Chained by my side and devoted to only one man — me.

Will Diana react? She is hopelessly in love with Mario, and everything she does is for his benefit. What will happen when I set the cat among the rats? Who will win? It had better be me.

More than anything, I want to make them suffer for what

they did to me and my family. The fact my father was blown sky high along with my sister has me looking in their direction for answers. Was this something they engineered? I wouldn't put it past them because my father's throne is obviously the prize in a very deadly game of chess.

Once again, we take our seats on my private jet and I leave Abigail on her own and head to the rear of the aircraft with Cesare.

In no time, we dive deep into the bottle of whiskey and Cesare raises his glass to me.

"Congratulations."

"Thank you." My smug grin causes him to laugh softly before he pulls out his phone and shows me a text he received when I was at the chapel.

"Interesting."

I raise my eyes to his and he nods, a thoughtful expression on his face.

"Do you think she knows who this is?"

"There's only one way to find out. May I?"

I reach for his phone, and he nods, watching me leave with a considered expression as I head to the front of the plane.

* * *

ABIGAIL LOOKS WRECKED as she slumps in her seat, still wearing the wedding dress, her eyes closed and her skin as pale as a white lily. For a moment, I stand and feast my eyes upon a beauty I wasn't expecting to call my wife, and doubt I'll ever tire of seeing that face.

Her porcelain skin and plump ruby red lips are just too tempting and those astonishing green eyes closed against the fiery gleam in them she wears so well. Her hair is sandy but highlighted with several shades, all complementing one another as they shine like a halo around her head. Her body is svelte with her curves in all the right places, the skin soft and stretched like silk over her long shapely limbs. She has been crafted from my sinful dreams and I long to ruin every single inch of her and almost as if she senses the approaching danger, her eyes snap open and she hisses, "Fucking pervert."

"Why?" I'm amused at the fight in her as she huffs, "Staring at me like a peeping tom. What's the matter? Don't you have any puppy dogs to pull the tails off?"

"Just for your information…" I sit in the seat opposite and lean forward. "I hate animal cruelty and if I come across it, I fucking kill the bastard responsible."

For a moment, her lips twitch and her expression softens, and then she mumbles, "That's good to know."

"Do you know this man?" I waste no time studying her reaction as she stares at the small screen.

For a moment, she doesn't react and then she leans forward and peers a little closer. "I think I've seen him before. How old is this?"

"I'm guessing it must be thirty years old, give or take a few years."

She studies it harder. "Is that Judge Stevenson?"

I nod. "Standing by your father's side, as usual."

"This man." She points to the man on the other side of her father. "He looks familiar."

I hold my breath as she studies it harder and then shakes her head. "I've seen that face before, but I can't place it. Do you know his name?"

I do, but I'm not ready to reveal that yet and I shrug. "No."

She bites her lip in concentration and there is something about her that's confusing my emotions. Possibly it's because she's wearing that fucking wedding dress and looking so edible, I want to wolf her down whole.

In fact, after the sweetest kiss in the car, I have an increasing urge to carry on with that, which is inconvenient because I don't want to catch feelings for this woman. I want to break her, but to do that I need to make her fall in love with me. More for Mario's benefit than mine, and so I switch my approach and soften my voice.

"Does it hurt?"

I glance down and love the way her cheeks flush with color as I reference her ass. She shifts slightly and as she winces, I have my answer.

"I can help with that?"

"You've done enough." She rolls her eyes and I grin, snapping my fingers so my attendant comes running.

"Bring my wife some pain killers and hot tea."

Abigail looks up and shakes her head slightly.

"What?" I laugh softly.

She studies me hard.

"You. One minute you act like a beast and the next you're fucking Prince Charming. I don't know which one I'll get next."

"Are you complaining?"

"Of course, I'm fucking complaining. You're not really selling marriage to you."

"What would you prefer, princess? A vanilla husband who treats you with kid gloves. Someone who places you high on a pedestal and worships you from below. A man like Jefferson, perhaps, who acts a certain way with you and then screws around behind your back in the filthiest of ways."

I lean forward. "When he returns to your bed at night, you'll always wonder where he's been. As he fucks you, you won't know if his cock has been used already that day and what sewer he put it in. Your life will be built on lies and one-way mirrors. You will become disillusioned and seek membership to clubs like the Banned Room. You'll both lead separate lives and put on a united front of respectability."

"Are you saying life with you would be different from that?"

She leans closer and I feel her breath as she whispers, "What would marriage be like with you, Matteo?"

Hearing my name fall from her lips is not unpleasant and she whispers huskily, "I'm certain you just described your own version of marriage. Endless whores and broken promises. Using your wife like a sex toy and then leaving her to be grateful for that while you carry on with your day. Marriage to you would suck, which is why I'm glad this is a temporary arrangement and I'm the lucky one who will walk away and take charge of my own life when you've got what you want."

She leans back and stares at me with a hint of triumph and it makes me smile, something that obviously takes her by surprise.

She's even more surprised when I move and take the seat beside her and turn her face to mine, loving how her beautiful eyes sparkle with lust.

Leaning forward, I rest my lips against hers and whisper, "What if I never let you go?"

She pulls back with a start, and I tighten my grip, forcing her to stare into my eyes.

"What if you're everything I've ever wanted in a wife, and I decide to keep you?"

I dip in and suck her lower lip into my mouth and bite down gently, her small groan adding fuel to the fire as I set my tongue free inside her mouth, sweeping it against hers, wrapping it in possession, capturing her soft moans and locking them inside.

As I kiss my wife, I find one taste is just not enough, which surprises me. I don't kiss women; I fuck them and I never realized how much pleasure a simple kiss can give you. Even when I fucked Diana, kissing didn't mean much. It was always a good hard fuck somewhere hidden, and I suppose that was part of the excitement. Abigail, however, is the sweetest treat that a man like me is told to stay away from. Respectable, an all-

American girl, destined for greatness and life in a gilded cage. Heading up charity fundraisers and bearing the next generation of politicians and businessmen. If she has daughters, they will be raised in her image to be every bit as entitled as she is.

That is what makes her the sweetest treat to enjoy because it's forbidden to a man like me and I suppose that's the attraction for her too. One wild dance with the local bad boy to pack away in her memory box so she can remember the one time in her life she veered off the rails.

CHAPTER 12

ABIGAIL

I can't help myself. I want him so badly. It's like the worst he treats me, the more I want him, telling me I must have been a masochist in a previous life because the harder it is, the more it turns me on.

His gentle kisses are at odds with his treatment of me and right at this moment, I am happy to enjoy some tenderness for once. I've kissed men before, but nothing like this. I'm astonished how my desire drips beneath me and my heart races and my body gravitates to his, desperate for whatever contact it can get. The way my mind races as I consider the possibilities and, more than anything, the need to be naked and restrained while he dominates my body.

Last night showed me a world I want to explore at my leisure. The fact it was dark, and I was face down and tied to a bench, stripped away any shame I had. At that moment I was free, which is a joke when you consider the position I was in. It was as if it wasn't real and there were no repercussions. Nobody knew who I was, and I could walk away knowing I may never see them again. Sex with a stranger was liberating, but knowing it was sex with *him* took it to a whole different level.

Now I'm keen to revisit the experience and so, as he kisses me, I give him back more. I want him to ruin me for any other man because the men in my life are nothing like him. Safe, boring and manipulative. Respectable on the outside, but rotten to the core. Matteo wears that badge with pride for all to see, his danger evident for the world to shy away from. I am dancing close to the flame, and I love it when it burns, so I whisper against his lips, "Just so you know, you don't scare me."

His soft laugh rests against my lips and he whispers huskily, "Then you're a fool."

"Maybe."

I grin as he whispers, "I will ruin you, Abigail Kensington."

"I can't fucking wait, Mr. Ortega."

His low laugh makes me smile and I'm almost disappointed when he pulls away and stares at me long and hard. If anything, his expression is confused and I note the shutters come down as he says roughly, "Get some sleep."

He stands and heads to the rear of the aircraft, leaving me with a warm glow inside. Yes, Matteo Ortega may think he has the measure of me, but he didn't count on one thing. I'm loving every second of this and whatever he does in the name of breaking me will in fact have the opposite effect. He will empower me because I never liked the old me anyway, and it's time to break her apart and rebuild her stronger, more in control and a woman who knows her own mind and doesn't do anything just because she's told to.

* * *

Matteo leaves me alone for the rest of the flight and I use my time to discard the dress and freshen up in the insane bathroom that is the height of luxury on a plane. When I study my reflection, I note the difference almost immediately.

The eyes that stare back at me are bright and full of life. The slight flush to my skin was placed there by the man outside and, if I'm not mistaken, I appear more confident and less jaded.

Is this what happens when a girl becomes a woman? Something inside her switches and she is at peace with the world. I've changed and I'm giving full credit for that to my new husband because from the moment I met him, I felt a connection I'm keen to explore further.

Even when the stranger took me into that room, I was prepared to do anything to sate the thirst my meeting with Matteo had stirred. I was even picturing him in the man's place, and I wonder if my experience would have been as memorable if I had allowed that man to strip me of my innocence.

But it wasn't him. Matteo came for me, telling me it's doubtful I will do anything he's not aware of. He must have followed me and decided to take advantage of my weakness. What he doesn't know is the weakness in me was my virginity. Now it's gone, it's unleashed a power I never knew I had and far from fearing what happens next, I crave it.

Using the toilet as a seat, I contemplate my next move. It's obvious his intentions toward me are dishonorable. He needs me for something, and I wonder if it concerns the man in the photograph I saw on his phone. My father, Judge Stevenson, and a familiar face that I can't quite place. There's also the fact my father allowed me to walk away with him. That alone raised the red flags and I wonder what the bigger picture is here.

Then there's Matteo Ortega. A man who makes my pulse race and my demons scream inside me. He has set them free to wreak havoc on my world.

My thoughts inevitably turn to Jefferson, and I shiver. The image of him and that whore will never leave me. One thing's definite, when and if I make it back, I'm not agreeing to marry that bastard if it's the last thing I do. I'd rather make my own way in life and cut myself off from the billions my father keeps me compliant with. Surely there's more to life than money and since meeting Matteo, I have never felt so alive.

So, I stand and regard the woman looking back at me and smile.

I'm going to have my fun while I can and discover just what Abigail Kensington is made of.

* * *

HE IS WAITING when I exit the bathroom, leaning against the wall with a nonchalant smile.

"Going somewhere, princess?"

"You tell me." I make to pass, and he steps in front of me and pushes me back inside the small space. My back hits the basin and the storm in his eyes makes me swallow hard as he steps in front of me and kicks my legs apart, settling between them as if he holds that right.

"What are you doing?" I hiss and he reacts fast by gripping the back of my head and fisting my hair.

"I'm consummating our marriage."

"What, here?"

I stare at him in disbelief and his eyes glitter as he whispers huskily, "Why not?"

"Because I told you this arrangement was in name only, you bastard."

He chuckles against my neck.

"Oh yes, I remember your parting shot as you stormed from my office right into my sex club."

He nuzzles my neck and whispers, "Perhaps you prefer the darkness and the thrill of sex with a stranger."

I can't help it. His words leave me panting and as he rips off his tie, I hold my breath as he fastens it around my eyes.

He whispers huskily, "Turn around."

I don't even fight because this is exactly what I want and he pushes me hard against the basin, my head hitting the mirror as he inches my dress around my waist and rips off my panties, whispering, "You are soaked, princess. Like every wet dream I ever had."

I hear a zipper and the butterflies in my stomach take flight as his throbbing cock presses against my pussy.

He caresses my ass and then my clit and I moan against the hard surface as he growls, "Is this what you want, princess?"

"Yes." My voice is heavy with desire, and I want him so badly I can't think of anything else and then he teases my opening, causing me to moan softly.

As he pushes in, his hand lays flat against my mouth, stifling the groan that I can't keep inside.

He slides in fully, filling me, my walls stretching to allow him full access. He fists my hair and pushes in and out, slowly and leisurely, as if he has all day. The fact I can't see him is intoxicating because now I am free. I'm in my own sordid world of depravation and nobody can witness how much I love it. He is behind me and can't stare into my lust-filled eyes as he takes something from me I am eager to give.

As I come apart, my body sags and his stifled groan tells me he's come hard. Briefly, I wonder if he used protection. Not that it matters. I've been on contraception since puberty at my mother's insistence. There will be no unwanted babies in the Kensington household. Only ones ordered from the most prestigious donor. It makes me laugh that she considers that man to be Jefferson Stevenson, and I can only imagine the horror on her face if she could see me now.

CHAPTER 13

MATTEO

Just one taste, that's all it will take. I told myself that when I left her after the most surprising kiss of my life. Her lips have branded me and when I attempted to discuss business with Cesare, all I could think of was my wife. Perhaps it's that word that's changed everything. I've never had one before and to tell the truth, it was the last thing I wanted. But Abigail is different from anyone I've ever met, and a hard drug I can't get enough of. Her anger, her flippant words and her fire all combine in an addictive cocktail. I had to have more, but what happened in this bathroom hasn't even come close to sating the hunger I have for this woman.

The more time I spend with her, the more depraved I want to be. She matches me because she gets off on domination. I couldn't have wished for a better wife, and I am keen to test her limits back at my mansion.

As I come hard, I swear I see heaven, which is an interesting place for the devil in me. It feels so good, so addictive and as she slumps against me, I am so not done with her yet.

I leave the blindfold in place, and spin her around, growling, "Get on your knees."

She doesn't even question me and as I sit on the toilet seat, I place my hand on the top of her head, loving the submissive pose that belies the woman on her knees before me. Yes, this will be interesting because I want Mario to see that Abigail is fully under my command. That she will do anything I ask and subsequently I need to prepare her for what that means.

I growl, "Open your mouth."

She doesn't even hesitate, and I thrust two fingers inside and say roughly, "Suck them."

As she sucks my fingers, I experience a great sense of pride because this is exactly what I had planned. Despite her fire and hard words, she's a kitten inside and obviously gets off on this as much as I do.

I pull them out and stand, zipping up my pants, leaving her kneeling on the floor.

Then I leave the room without another word, interested to see what she does next.

I lock the door on my way out and catch sight of the attendant and growl, "Nobody goes in there."

He nods and quickly turns away, knowing not to question me.

I head off to find Cesare feeling in a much better mood than earlier, knowing that my wife is my perfect dream.

"Boss." He nods as I take the seat opposite and glance at my watch.

"How much longer?"

"Half an hour."

"Good." I'm keen to get Abigail back to my mansion and as the flight attendant appears, I snap, "Coffee please."

He heads off and Cesare laughs softly. "How's married life?"

I grin. "Exceptional."

He nods and says with interest. "What do you think the connection is?"

He holds up the picture on his phone and I shake my head.

"School perhaps. They are of that age. Do some digging into their past. Trace their education, friends, childhood addresses. Contact their friends, discover their past, and that should be enough to tell us what we know."

"Do you think it's connected with Abigail?"

He asks the one question that's been bugging me, and I say slowly. "It probably has *everything* to do with her. Think about it. Three men who have a connection. Now look at the next generation and I'm guessing you'll find the answer there. The only thing I don't get is why?"

Cesare nods, deep in concentration, swirling his whiskey around the cut glass as he considers the puzzle.

"Perhaps she can help when she recognizes the third man."

"*If* she recognizes him." I take the coffee the attendant hands me and consider my next move. Maybe I should wait a few more days before going in for the kill. Gather the information I need before making a mess of something I don't fully understand.

A few days teaching my wife how to please her husband is not an unpleasant use of my time, so I smile and say with satisfaction. "I will wait until you discover the facts."

Cesare nods. "I'll start as soon as we land."

As the jet begins its descent, I'm of the same mind. However, I won't need to wait until we land.

I finish the coffee and head to the bathroom, hoping I like what I see when I open the door.

As I peer into the small space, I smile. Such a good girl.

She is exactly where I left her. Blindfolded and kneeling, waiting for instruction.

She jumps as I bark, "Stand up." As she does, I reach for the blindfold and pull her dress down, rearranging it, minus her panties.

Her eyes blink against the harsh lighting and I say softly,

"You have pleased me, Miss. Kensington. Or should I say, Mrs. Ortega?"

Her breath hitches and her eyes cloud with lust and just like that, I want her again. It surprises me, so I say roughly, "Now go and take your seat for landing."

She scurries off and I glance at my reflection in the mirror and note a different look in my eye. I move across and stare at a man who has lost the bitter expression and appears almost animated. There can only be one reason for that – the game. I love this shit, and she is proving a worthy opponent. Will she complete the course, or will she fail? I'm more interested in that than defeating my stepmother, which surprises me more than anything.

Tearing my attention back to business, I crush my desire for my wife with an iron fist. I will *not* let her weaken me. She is a project, a means to an end, and I *will* send her back to her future without me in it.

I head outside the bathroom and purposefully join Cesare at the rear of the aircraft because I need distance from the woman who is shaping up to be even more manipulative than my stepmother.

CHAPTER 14

ABIGAIL

I'm still shaking after what happened in that bathroom. I loved it. The power of the man and the way I emptied my mind and allowed him to control me. It turned me on, and the bastard doesn't even realize how much. He believes he's humiliating me. That only happens when someone does something against their will. I want this. If anything, I am using him to get off, a thought that makes me smile as I picture him as a human vibrator.

* * *

WHEN THE AIRCRAFT LANDS, I wait for instruction. I am interested to learn what he has planned next, and I hate that I'm hoping it involves more of the same. I am fast becoming addicted to the freedom sex gives me. I tell myself he could be anyone. The nearest port in a storm and, if not him, then anyone else. But I'm only kidding myself. He is the reason I love it. Knowing it's him makes it more pleasurable and the fact we're married doesn't even bother me anymore.

For a brief second back in Vegas, it bothered me a lot. The

fact he gave me no choice and ordered me to marry him caused the anger to fire up my soul. Then I saw him, waiting by the altar, like every fantasy I ever had. A dark presence completely out of place in the chapel, as if God was about to strike him down for daring to think he had the right to walk inside. Then, when he watched me approach, I felt his dark stare consume me and beckon my soul from my body to his. I belong to him now. That's the message he gave me, and his subsequent actions demonstrated I was right and, for some fucked up reason, I liked it.

Belonging to a man like that is intoxicating—for me, anyway. When I imagine my future bridegroom watching me walk toward him, it leaves me cold. Jefferson Stevenson is nowhere near the man Matteo Ortega is and never will be. Dark, dangerous and deadly. Qualities I shouldn't crave but can't help myself. I am drawn to the darkness and crave it with a thirst that nothing can sate. However, he is a problem that needs dealing with and that will be the first thing I tackle when we get to wherever the fuck he's taking me.

This time when I exit the aircraft, I am directed to the third car by an unknown face. One of the silent soldiers who accompanies us everywhere and there is no sign of my new husband or his constant companion.

As I take up my seat in the car, I am alone and as the cars move off, I imagine him in the car in front, plotting more humiliation to heap upon my already burdened shoulders.

I stare out at the familiar landscape and realize we're in New York. I have been here many times because my father owns a penthouse in Manhattan that we visit often.

We pass the familiar streets, and I'm excited to see where we're heading.

The cars turn off fifth avenue into the underground car park of a superior apartment block.

As they come to a stop, my door remains closed for at least five minutes before Cesare opens it and peers inside.

"Mrs. Ortega." He says reverently, indicating I should exit the car, and as I straighten up and stare around at the cold, bleak car park, I shiver inside. It's like a scene from The Sopranos, because there are men in black everywhere, their expressions set in stone. I can't even locate the bastard I call husband and wonder if this is just another one of his games.

Cesare directs me to an elevator and, as we step inside, he presses the light for the penthouse, and I resist rolling my eyes and maintain a blank expression.

The air is thick with unspoken words as we make the journey at opposite ends of the elevator and as it stops and the doors open, I regard a modern apartment in neutral colors that appears to survey the whole of the State.

"Mr. Ortega has requested that you remain here until he comes for you."

I nod and wait for him to walk away before I venture into the apartment. I'm no stranger to wealth. This is similar to my father's apartment, but for some reason it surprises me that he has the same taste. I'm not sure what I was expecting really, but, in my mind, I suppose I imagined darkened walls and chrome and steel. This is minimalist and chic, and I like it a lot.

I move across to the wall where a table stands, holding a tray of spirits, and I help myself to a glass of red wine from the decanter. I may as well make myself at home, so I take it across to the window and look down on the skyline. It's certainly impressive and I note the blue sky and trees in full leaf in the park below.

Freedom.

It's ironic that this is the most freedom I have ever felt now I'm away from under my mother's watchful eye. I briefly wonder if she is concerned for me at all, or just angry that her well-laid plans are not going as smoothly as she wanted them to.

"Abigail."

His voice slides down my shivering back and grips my heart, squeezing it until the life flashes before my eyes.

I turn slowly and regard a man who Satan carved in his image as he stands watching me from a door set at one end of the apartment.

"Matteo." I raise my glass to him in a mock salute and love how his eyes glitter with danger as he shifts off the wall.

Before he can even speak, I set the glass down on the table and stare at him defiantly.

"I have a business proposition for you."

I say firmly, and he raises his eyes.

"So, you're suddenly in business now."

His smirk makes me shrug and I take the seat at one end of the table, pointing to the vacant chair at the other end.

"I am now in the business of being your wife."

I regard him coolly and his amused smirk gives him a lightness I wasn't expecting.

He takes the seat and leans forward, his arms on the table as he stares. at me with a great deal of interest flashing in his turbulent eyes.

"I take it you have some demands."

He appears more interested than annoyed, and I nod, maintaining a cool, detached expression.

"You are a man who uses guns and sex as weapons where words would be more effective."

"Is that so?"

He laughs softly. "I haven't heard you complaining yet. In fact–"

He casts his eyes the length of me and grins wickedly, "I'm guessing you've loved every minute of it so far."

"I have." I fire back and his eyes widen a little, telling me I've surprised him.

I shrug and study my perfectly manicured fingernail.

"You see, Matteo, you have given me something I've wanted for some time. Freedom."

He raises his eyes and I nod. "Despite your pathetic attempts at dominating me, they have only worked because I like it. You may have control of my body, but you will never control my mind and what's in there isn't as compliant as you thought it was."

"I see." He leans back and rubs his finger against his chin, his eyes flashing as he stares at me hard.

"So, here is the deal. It's obvious you need me for something, and I doubt it's merely to fuck and humiliate me, no matter how much I'm enjoying that, by the way."

He smirks and if anything, he likes what I'm saying due to the amusement on his lips and the lust in his eyes.

"You showed me a photograph on the plane."

He sits up straighter as I say thoughtfully, "The face was familiar, but I can't remember a name. The fact that my father allowed you to, shall we say, employ me, tells me it fits with his own plans."

"Do you know what they are?"

Matteo says with interest, and I shake my head.

"Not yet, but if we work together and pool our knowledge, I'm sure we can figure it out."

"Is that your business proposition?"

He appears almost disappointed, and I smile, leaning forward and fixing him with a lust-filled gaze.

"My proposition is this. In return for assisting you in whatever game you're playing, I want you to teach me everything about domination."

He is surprised. I can tell by the jerk of his head and the shock that lights his eyes.

"Why?" He appears confused, and I shrug.

"Maybe when you showed me the video of Jefferson, it unlocked a dark part of my soul. I loved it. I liked it so much I couldn't think of anything else. It turned me on and when I went to the club, it was to discover it for myself. I have so many questions and so much I need to discover because when I return home, I will take charge of my life. I need you to build my confidence. Strip away my defenses and recreate me into a confident woman who can take on the world."

For a moment he says nothing and just scratches his jaw carefully with consideration and then he says in a softer voice, "You don't need my help for that."

"But I do."

I stand and move to join him and, to his surprise, kneel before him, taking his hands in mine and whispering, "With you I can be anything. You won't judge me; you won't think I'm a freak and you won't use it against me."

"How can you be so sure of that, given the circumstances that brought you here?"

I smile up at him and already have my answer when I note the expression in his eyes.

"Because you want me too and at the end of this, you will have a hard time letting me go."

He reaches out and places his finger under my chin and tips my face to his and the danger flashes in his eyes as he says roughly, "You are correct. I want you, but I *will* let you go."

"Do we have a deal, sir?"

My lashes flutter as he rubs his thumb against my lips and I say softly, "Tell me your reasons for using me and I'll help anyway I can, in return for everything you can teach me about sex."

If I was embarrassed once, I'm definitely not now because this man has unleashed the emotion inside me that doesn't give a fuck and yet I'm surprised when he reaches down and takes my hand and pulls me up with him.

His hand slides around my waist, his other hand reaching around my back, he pulls me close and whispers against my ear, "You have a deal, Mrs. Ortega. Now, what do you want first? Information, or an orgasm. The choice is yours."

For some reason that makes me giggle and as I gaze into his eyes, I almost see amusement there and I lightly touch my lips to his and whisper, "Business first. Tell me who that man is, and I may be able to help."

The fact his hand is caressing my ass makes me regret my choice and when he pulls away and points to the chair I vacated, he says firmly, "Then sit and I'll tell you everything I know."

CHAPTER 15

MATTEO

She has surprised me again. It's not often the tables turn on me, but I'm intrigued. Far from breaking this woman, it appears that every harsh word and crude act makes her stronger, which interests me way more than I'll ever let on. I've never met a woman like Abigail Kensington and I'm more impressed with every sentence she speaks. I always prided myself on being an enigma, but she broke the mold when she was born. Cool, detached and regal, yet with the mind and body of a whore. A cunning woman using her power to get what she wants and who wouldn't be impressed by that? Used and manipulated wisely, she could become my best asset, and I lied to her when I said I would let her go. That is looking more unlikely after every word that spills from those luscious lips. With every sentence she is adding another chain to her leash and it's now doubtful I will ever return her.

Marriage to this woman may have been out of a desire to infuriate Mario Bachini, but it's worked to my advantage because now she is mine whether she likes it or not.

"The man in the picture is called Sam Bachini."

I study her reaction and I am not disappointed.

The shock on her face is replaced with fear and her previous bravado deserts her in seconds.

"Sam." Her voice shakes as I nod, interested in her reaction.

"You may remember his son, Mario."

If anything, she looks as if she's going to hurl and slumps back in her seat and says with a quivering voice. "Please tell me this doesn't concern that family."

"Why not?"

She appears almost desperate as she says fearfully. "I met them once at a party they threw at their home."

"Go on."

I listen with interest and Abigail shivers. "It was unusual for us to go. Mom wasn't keen, even though it was her friend we were visiting."

"Not your father's?"

"No. I didn't even realize they had met before. Anyway, mom told us we only had to show our faces and leave and then my father told me to stay away from their son Mario."

"Why would he do that?"

"I'm not sure but mom interrupted and told my father they should have left me at home."

"What did he say?"

"They had requested my attendance."

I sense the anger balling inside me and snap, "What happened when you arrived?"

"My father was asked to accompany Sam to his office. It was as if they had business to attend to. His mother pulled Mario forward and told him to take care of me, but my father snapped and told me I must remain with my mom. They didn't allow me to mix with the opposite sex."

"I see."

I settle down knowing she was spared that particular pleasure and Abigail shivers. "I felt his interest. Even though I was sixteen and hadn't met many guys before, I could tell he had plans for me. When I left, he was standing beside a girl around the same age as me. She was a pretty blonde, and it was obvious she hated me on sight."

"My stepmother." I growl and Abigail stares at me with astonishment.

"How?"

"Diana came into our home at my father's invitation. Our mother had died, and she was her replacement."

"Surely not." Abigail is shocked and I don't blame her, and snarl, "That woman is pure evil. She seduced me and my two brothers and then chose our father. He sent us away, and she moved her 'brother' Mario Bachini in to take our place. He became my father's consigliere and now they want the Ortega empire."

"That's disgusting."

"Which part?"

I sigh heavily. "We need to bring them down and take back control. The reason you are here is because Mario has an interest in you that was never realized."

"So, I'm your weapon against him." She shakes her head. "Not much of a plan, is it?"

For some reason, that makes me laugh and my admiration for this woman increases tenfold.

"Who knows?" I shrug. "The fact your father obviously knew Sam already throws a little light on the subject. Now we need to discover what their friendship involved before we can use the information against our enemies."

"And me. What were you planning?"

"To watch Mario's reaction when I brought you home. To see what he would do when it was obvious I was treating you like my fucking whore, knowing he could do nothing because you were my wife."

She shakes her head and laughs softly. "Like I said, it's not much of a plan, is it?"

She sighs heavily and picks up her discarded wine glass.

"We need to find the connection. You are right about that. If it's any help, I will play my part. I'll do whatever you require, but it will be on the understanding I'm loving it."

I chuckle softly and this is the moment I believe I fall in love with Abigail Ortega. We are two like-minded souls, and it will be my pleasure to drag her into my dark world. However, somebody should have told her to be careful what you wish for because she doesn't realize what she's just taken on.

"Anything else you can tell me?" I fix her with a dark look and she shakes her head, noting the shift in the atmosphere. It's as if I'm dragging all the oxygen out of the room as I stare at her hard and the way her eyes light up tells me she's understood the situation perfectly.

"Then come here." I say, beckoning her toward me with a blank expression.

I watch her chest heave as she pushes back her chair and heads my way.

As she reaches me, I spin her around, so she is facing the table and growl, "Bend over. Arms flat on the table." She does as I say, and it takes me back to the club and the last time she was in this position. The fact we are in a room that anyone could walk into makes me wonder if she'll go through with this. She doesn't know that my staff are under strict instructions not to enter the apartment until I say so, and so I remove my belt, the sound of which causes her to moan softly.

As I position behind her, I push her dress around her waist and wrap the belt around her throat, fastening it like a collar, holding the slack like a leash. Then I pull her head up with the belt and whisper, "Do you want me to control you, princess?"

"Yes, sir."

I smooth my hand on her shapely ass and she purrs like a kitten. Then I whisper close to her ear, "Empty your mind."

She pants as the anticipation builds and I unzip my pants,

the noise the only one in the room. As I settle between her ass, I say huskily, "Is this what you want? To be fucked from behind like a common whore?"

"Yes."

Her voice is needy and so turned on it makes me smile. Who would have thought this American princess was hiding the morals of a gutter whore inside?

I pull up on the belt, causing her to gasp as I push in hard and with every thrust I make, I pull the leash and she moans as I take her from behind.

Her body slides against the polished table as I punish her for daring to challenge me and just before she cums, I pull out and slap her ass hard, causing her to gasp, "What the…?"

I spin her around and pull the belt until her lips are close to mine and I hiss, "Nobody controls me. I don't give you what you want because you demand it. You earn it first."

Her eyes are wide and full of shock as I release her and she falls back onto the table and as I zip up my pants, she hisses, "You fucking bastard."

"Get used to it, princess, because you're married to me now."

I can tell she was so close to the edge because her cheeks are flushed and her breath comes in pants and I say casually, "Just so you understand, this is all on my terms. You will get your wish, but it may not be quite what you had in mind."

I turn and walk to the door I entered through and say roughly, "Follow me. There was a reason I made you wait there. I needed to prepare the surprise I have for you."

I hear her shuffling off the table and hide the smirk that will tell her how amused she makes me. She needs to fear me, and what I have in mind is the perfect way of achieving that.

She catches me up as I head through the door and as we walk to the end of the hallway, I wonder if she'll be so brave when she sees what's inside the room at the end.

As I turn the lock, she is at my shoulder and as she follows me inside, her gasp of horror makes me hard.

"What is this place?"

"Your fucking dream, princess."

"Are you sure about that?" She sounds completely horrified and I nod as I turn and watch her reaction first hand.

Like the Banned Room, this room is kitted out for every sexual perversion possible and unlike the Banned Room, this one is not designed for comfort. This is no red room, this is a prison, and Abigail's eyes widen as she takes it all in.

"Tell me about it." Once again, she surprises me as she walks around the room, touching the stone walls where iron cuffs hang, offering no comfort.

"It's a dungeon of sorts." I perch on the bench in the center of the room, and she replies harshly, "I can see that. Why is it so cold?"

"Because it's not designed for comfort."

"I can see that."

She turns to look at me and surprises me again by grinning.

"When do we start?"

I shake my head and laugh out loud, causing her to say irritably, "Is something amusing you, husband?" She says the word sarcastically and my palm itches to put her in her place.

"You amuse me, princess. I never realized you were so, shall we say, adventurous? It appears I've opened Pandora's box where you're concerned."

For some reason, that makes her smile, and she glances around with interest.

"I never knew I had it in me."

Just seeing her standing in my den of sin makes me proud somehow. I never expected to feel anything, but I'm fast realizing the value of her. It's one thing dominating a submissive, even better when it fills them with horror, but Abigail is a challenge I wasn't expecting because whatever I do, I'm convinced it won't be enough where she's concerned.

It intrigues me, so I nod to the door and say in a warmer voice, "We will revisit this place later. Come, we should eat first."

The disappointment on her face causes an ache in my heart that is alien to me. I don't like seeing her upset. I like to see her smile. The fact I even care what she's feeling is surprising me – a lot. More than anything, I want to test her limits, but I need to understand what has driven her to this point first. She is hiding something deep inside and until I learn what that is, the games will be put on hold. I need to know her mind before her body so I can make this good for her. One step out of line and I could destroy her forever, so as painful as it is, sex with Abigail will have to be put on hold.

CHAPTER 16

ABIGAIL

I am so disappointed. That room was fresh out of my nightmares and something I crave more than my dreams right now. I was so close to losing my mind back there and that's the attraction. I want to lose who I am because I don't like her very much.

Abigail Kensington is weak, controlled, and subservient. She does everything her parents tell her and they would never tell her to do this.

That's the attraction. My rebellion, of sorts. I will be doing something that would cause my mom a panic attack and I'd love every minute of it. Sex makes me a different person entirely. A wanton woman with no code to follow, no rules, and a chance to fling decency from the window. The antithesis of who I am most of the time and this room is the extreme of that.

I want to know what it's like to be chained naked to a cold stone wall and tortured sexually. I want it to hurt and experience the pain with the pleasure. It will drive out those demons that live inside me so they can't hurt me anymore. I will always have my depravations to cling to when faced with my upstanding life.

Now I know why Jefferson did it. It makes me understand him a little more. Would it be the same with him? Of course not. We are too alike.

It must be Matteo Ortega because he has danger tattooed on his soul. I need a black heart to rub off on mine and make me stronger.

I follow him from the room, wishing like hell we didn't need to eat. Why do I want this so much? I can't explain that to myself and I'm surprised when he leads me to a small dining room that overlooks the skyline and says softly, "Please, take a seat. I've had dinner prepared; my chef will deliver it personally."

I sit opposite him, and he pours us both a glass of wine and as I sip the deep spicy liquid, it warms my blood.

We say nothing and sip our wine as soft, melodic music spills from hidden speakers. It's classical, which surprises me. I never had this man down as an educated one and yet it's the perfect accompaniment to my mood.

It calms me yet adds drama to an occasion that doesn't really need it.

The door opens and the chef wheels in a trolley and we sit in silence as he places domed dishes on the table before us. He sets some plates down and half bows before leaving and I raise my eyes as soon as the door closes.

"Who do you think you are, Matteo? A king perhaps?"

He chuckles softly. "Of sorts."

"Then you're deluded."

I shake my head as he lifts off the domes one by one and I see a feast before me fit for the king he thinks he is.

There are so many decadent dishes my mouth waters and as we help ourselves and load the food onto our plates, I relax for the first time since I met him.

This is almost normal, and I like it.

"Tell me about your life, princess."

He regards me through those decadent eyes, and I feel a flutter inside that only he can create.

"Pampered, spoiled, controlled, take your pick. Everything you believe I am is probably right."

I raise my glass of wine to him in a salute and sigh.

"To everyone outside looking in, I have it all. The only child of a billionaire given everything money can buy. The trouble is, I can't move without my parents' blessing. My days are controlled with classes, sports and practicing accomplishments. At night I am wheeled out to functions and listen while my life is mapped out before me."

"So, you had no choice regarding your impending engagement?"

"None at all. I was told over Sunday lunch that I would be getting engaged to Jefferson Stevenson. He would make a fine husband and I should count myself lucky. One day he will be a respected Judge like his father, and I'll be expected to be the best wife possible to back him up."

I sigh heavily and shiver a little. "Children, charity functions, entertain his associates and form friendships with like-minded couples. The American dream. You'll find that description on the box but when you open it there's not a lot of worth inside."

"And you think my life is a bed of roses?"

He shakes his head as I stare at him in surprise.

"You do what you want. You've demonstrated that."

"Is that what you think?"

He laughs and raises his glass to mine.

"My life is no less controlled than yours. As soon as I could walk, I was taught to fight. As soon as I could speak, I was beaten if I spoke out of turn. The only education I had was in fighting, extortion and pain. I watched my mother murdered in cold blood before my eyes and my father was the killer. I was seduced by a woman who played on my need for love and kindness and turned it against me. Everything I have has been hard won and I am always looking over my shoulder for the hit man who follows me everywhere. My life will be short and depraved, so it's no wonder I get my kicks from torturing people who I consider have it better than me."

The expression in his eyes should scare me, but it turns me on. What can I say? I'm a hot mess.

The fact he's so broken intrigues me. A violent beginning has created a violent man, yet somehow, deep down inside, there is something that interests me more. A yearning for something he has never had. Like me, he is searching for that missing piece. He craves the light. I crave the darkness and when light meets dark, you get dusk. We are in that gray area searching for a rainbow. Which side it falls remains to be seen, but both of us want to discover the pot of gold at the end of it and for the first time since I met him, I fully understand the man I married.

"We can help one another." The words come out in a rush, and he nods.

"I thought that was the plan."

"No." I stand and head toward him, dropping to my knees and taking his hands in mine.

"We both have something the other person needs and maybe this is our time to swap desires. You want something you've never had and so do I."

I reach up and cup his face in my hand and stare deep into his eyes.

"Let me love you, Matteo."

I'm shocked when his expression changes and I note a vulnerability that wasn't there before and as he leans his face against my hand, I rub my thumb over the stubble on his jaw.

Then I push myself up and fasten my lips to his, kissing him softly, gently, with so much emotion it even shocks me.

This time, our kiss is gentle, probing and delicious. Feelings are released and the moans are for something sweet and forbidden until now.

This time I want to make love to my man, and I wonder if he'll allow that to happen.

His hand snaps against mine and he deepens the kiss. It becomes a hunger for something we have both been denied to this point.

I shift onto his lap and run my hand around the back of his head, this time holding him in place as I demonstrate how much I want him.

The clock ticking on the wall is in perfect time to my heartbeat and as he unzips my dress, I shrug off his jacket.

As the fabric falls, he runs his hand over my breast and edges the material aside, and I slip my hand inside his shirt and caress his toned abs. We are in no hurry to rush something that has been denied to us both until now and as we break the kiss, he whispers, "Come. I have something else to show you."

My dress remains on the floor, and I walk with my hand in his, dressed only in my underwear, but I'm not ashamed.

It's as if the world is empty and we are Adam and Eve. Alone in our version of paradise.

He leads me to a spiral staircase just outside the dining room and as we head up, I fully expect it to lead to his bedroom.

Instead, I blink in astonishment when he pushes a door open, and we step outside onto a roof terrace. The whole of New York lies as a carpet under our feet as we walk on toughened glass and it's as if we're walking on the clouds. There is a large hot tub bubbling away and comfortable sun loungers heaped with luxurious white cushions. He flicks a switch and lights set the place on fire as the fire pit bursts into life.

He holds my attention as he removes his shirt, staring into my eyes the entire time. His pants soon follow until he stands in his Calvin Klein's and, with a heated gaze in his eyes, he drops them too. I swallow hard when I regard my man for the first time, standing in naked splendor before me. His eyes glitter in the darkening light and my mouth dries as I run my tongue around my lips and, reaching behind me, unclasp my bra.

I step out of my panties and love his lustful expression as he reaches for my hand and leads me silently into the tub.

As the hot decadent bubbles surround us, he pulls me close and kisses me so deeply I forget to breathe.

Now we are naked, something that hasn't happened before, and as my breasts press against his chest, I moan with desire.

He rains light kisses over my face before trailing his lips down to my neck and I arch my back against the side of the tub as he lowers his mouth to my breast. As he sucks it in deep, a shiver passes through me, loving the emotions that are scattering my principles. I thought I wanted it rough, but this is exquisite. So many more feelings are involved as he worships my body in the open air.

He shifts so his back is to the tub and pulls me onto his lap, gripping my arms and staring deep into my eyes. As I feel his cock pressing against my lust crazed pussy, he whispers, "I'm going to make you mine."

I smile and fasten my lips to his and whisper, "I already am."

Then in one delicious moment he is inside me and I'm surprised at my reaction to that. This is so different, magical even, and as he moves slowly, he stares into my eyes with a promise. It's so intense and overwhelms me a little and as he increases the pace, he whispers, "Is that good, princess?"

I smile and moan softly, "Yes."

I'm not lying. It's better than I ever thought it would be and I'm disappointed when he pulls out suddenly.

"What...?" I'm confused, but he merely grins wickedly and pulls me from the tub, the cool air chilling my skin.

Leading me over to one of the sun loungers, he says huskily, "Lie back."

As my body meets the plump cushions, he drags my thighs apart and settles between them. His tongue flicking against my clit, causing me to cry out.

As he sucks it in, I shudder as the orgasm builds and he lifts his head and growls, "Not yet."

"I can't..."

"Not now!" he commands in a voice that tells me I had better listen, and I try to distract my mind from the intense pleasure it is experiencing now.

The fact he is feasting on my sin is enough to make me explode, but I try desperately hard to remain in control.

He pulls away and whispers, "Good girl."

I don't know why that's like receiving some kind of fucking medal, but I'm almost glowing at his praise.

I watch as he lies on the bed beside me and says roughly,

"I want to see those lips wrapped around my cock."

I scurry to my feet and this time I settle between his legs and take him in, loving how smooth he is against my tongue.

To be on all fours sucking his cock would be degrading if anyone could see, but for some reason it gives me a thrill. What if they're watching us now? It makes me groan out loud and his tortured ones meet mine as he thrusts deeper down my throat, causing me to gag a little.

Then he fists my hair and pushes in deeper, and it makes my eyes water as he pumps fast into my throat. It's almost painful and yet I love every second of it and am almost disappointed when he pulls out and says with a husky growl.

"Sit on me, princess. Show me what you like."

As I sit astride him, I revel in the moment when he enters my body. It's so good, so right and as flicks my clit, it sends me over the edge, and I come with the loudest scream all over his throbbing cock.

As I slump onto his body, he fists my hair and thrusts up inside me with a brutal force that has me gasping for air, and then he fills me completely with a loud roar and as his cum leaks from inside me, I couldn't give a fuck what happens next.

CHAPTER 17

MATTEO

What just happened took me completely by surprise. I've never had feelings before. Not even with Diana.

I wanted her, craved her even, but I never had an overwhelming need to protect her like I do my pretty princess.

I can't deal with it because for a moment there, I lost control. It was like an epiphany as my body experienced things it never has before. Emotion mingled with desire caused me to come so hard I almost blacked out.

It was special; she is special and as she slumps on my chest, I rain light kisses on her head and experience an overwhelming need to hold her close. Was that what they call making love? It feels that way, and yet how can a man like me ever love another? It's not in my DNA and yet it's different and I want to repeat the experience to test it was real.

My arms wrap around the soft body of the woman who surprises me more every minute I spend with her, and my heart pounds at the thought of never experiencing her. Never experiencing *this*.

I've had sex countless times, and domination is my

preferred method. Not this sweet loving that tells me I've missed something amazing, though picturing anyone else in her place fills me with distaste. It's Abi. She's the only one who matters now, and it amuses me how quickly things change.

She lifts her head and stares straight into my eyes and smiles. "Thank you."

I stroke her cheek softly. "It was my pleasure."

She giggles, and it makes me smile and she whispers, "That was the best one yet."

"It was."

She springs forward and kisses me slowly and as her tongue edges inside, my heart feels for once in its miserable life. She is everything I never knew I wanted and everything I will die to protect. I want to capture this emotion and hold it in an iron grip because now I've had one taste, I'm addicted.

She presses against me and says sexily, "Can we do that again?"

I laugh softly. "Of course. I insist on it, but first we have business to attend to."

She looks worried. "What business?"

Pulling her up to a sitting position, I wrap my arms around her and say with a sigh. "I told your father I required your assistance for charity work. Tonight, there is a gala at Madison Square Garden, and we're expected to attend."

"But..." she makes to protest, and I place my finger on her lips, effectively silencing her.

"We need to play the game. You accompany me, and we'll be photographed and all over the internet by morning. Your parents will see that you're ok and the whole of Washington will accept your internship."

"But what if word gets out that we're married?"

I wink and say with a chuckle. "That's what I'm counting on."

I pull her up before she can question me and as we walk

through the terrace naked and dirty, I congratulate myself on my quick thinking of making her my bride.

We shower together and more than anything I wish we had time for round two and three, but time is against us.

"What will I wear?" Abigail says as she watches me toweling off before the vanity unit.

"I've had a few dresses delivered. One of them should fit."

"I have a closet full of dresses in my father's apartment. We could go over there and select one."

"No time." I shrug as I flick a comb through my hair and say roughly, "You'll find what you need in the closet next to mine. You have twenty minutes."

She makes to argue, and I growl menacingly, "Unless you want me to punish you, I'd get a move on."

It makes me smile at the lust in her voice as she whispers, "Punish me?"

"Trust me, it won't be pleasant. So do as I say."

She lingers a little, causing me to sigh and say darkly, "If you don't want my belt on your ass, you'll move now."

She scrambles for the door, and I grin when she says as a parting shot, "And you call that a punishment."

As the door closes, I laugh to myself. How did I get so lucky?

As I dress, I think about the evening ahead. It was planned before my wedding. The usual charity shit I must do to remain respectable in a city that is anything but. To show my face and mix with New York's elite, dealing with the shit they shovel as part of their working day. Men want to strike deals with me to assure them of my protection, and their wives and girlfriends want to fuck me.

What can I say? Women seem to love a bad guy and I'm worse than most.

As I pull on my customary black suit and splash some aftershave, I have an interest in the evening ahead that isn't normally there. There is so much still to play for, and I wonder if I'm expecting too much of my wife. For a moment, I savor the sound of that word.

My wife.

I'm more surprised than anyone to find I'm happy about that. What started out as revenge has become everything to me and I'll end Mario Bachini's life if he even breathes the same air as her. Whatever he has planned will happen over my dead body because the thought of anyone ever touching my wife causes the blood lust to enter my heart. I will kill to protect what's mine and this time she is not getting away, despite the deal I made with her father. If Jefferson thinks he has a future with Abigail, he's about to learn a very hard lesson.

Somehow, my scheming backfired on me. She took everything I threw at her and tossed it back in my face, and then reached in and stole my heart when I wasn't looking. Perhaps it's because I'm a possessive bastard, or just a bastard, but she's my toy and I don't share.

I make my way into the living room and find Cesare waiting for me.

He holds out a whiskey and smirks.

"Good evening, boss."

"You could say that." I grin and he rolls his eyes.

"Then you're the lucky one." He sighs and I say with concern.

"Any news?"

"No."

Cesare chucks back the whiskey and I know it's disguising the pain. He met a woman six months ago, Stephanie, who was a waitress at one of the clubs. She was different from the others, and he soon made her his woman. He seemed happy for once. There was a difference to him that I am only just beginning to understand. Then one day she disappeared. No word on the street, nothing. Nobody could tell us what happened, and it's been driving him nuts. Cesare is a man who gets information from the unlikeliest places and even he can't discover her whereabouts. He won't stop trying, though, and I'll do everything possible to help him with that.

"Are we set for tonight?" I ask, hoping it's all in place.

"My contact assured me that Mario's and Diana's names are on the guest list."

"Anyone else we should know about?"

He sighs and I snap, "What?"

I stare at him with a piercing gaze as he falters and says with a sigh, "Demelza Gregory."

"Fuck."

I drain my glass and reach for another. "That's all I need."

Demelza is a woman who tries too hard. Mainly with me. It appears her sole aim in life is to be my girlfriend and despite the fact I treat her like shit, she keeps coming back for more. Her parents are well known in society, her father Preston Gregory is high up on the New York stock exchange and so morally corrupt he makes me look like Santa Claus.

"Keep her away from me." I growl and Cesare nods dutifully.

"Anything else to tell me?"

He shakes his head. "I'll head down and check everything's in place."

I nod as he leaves the room and, taking advantage of my privacy, I reach for my phone.

"Leo."

"Matteo. To what do I owe this call?"

Leonardo is my older brother and set on inheriting the title of Don Ortega from our father. This whole charade is to ensure that happens and I say with a sigh.

"Any news on the will?"

Our father's will is due to be read next week and we need to cast our eyes on it. If he left everything to Diana, our evil stepmother and Mario's whore, we are screwed. If he did, we need to re-write it and fast and Leo has been tasked with getting access to it.

"No, but I'm working on it."

"I hope you work fast because time is a luxury we don't have."

"What about you? Have you carried out your part of the plan?" he fires back, and I'm quite smug as I laugh softly.

"I have her and congratulations are in order."

There's a slight pause, and he laughs softly. *"You bastard."*

"Thank you." I swirl the contents of my glass around and enjoy a moment's satisfaction. My other brother, Domenico, was to find Diana's sister and use her much in the same way as I intended on using Abi. This time to bring Diana down and steal the money she stole from our father's bank account. Flora, Diana's sister, was to impersonate her and transfer the money to one of our bank accounts instead. It worked well and now we have the money that was stolen from us and the resources to control our empire. We only need to remove the current incumbents and life can get back to normal with an Ortega in charge.

Leo adds, *"I understand you're attending the gala tonight. Just a heads up that Jefferson Stevenson has been added to the guest list."*

My anger knows no limits because why the fuck didn't Cesare tell me that vital piece of information?

Leo must sense my anger and says quickly, *"It's just been added. I'm sure your consigliere will inform you."*

"How do you know already?"

It never ceases to amaze me that Leo knows things before any of us and I'm the one who's meant to be the information whizz.

"I have a contact at Madison Square Garden. I'm tracking a man called Mason Hargreaves. He's due to be there tonight and I want to know who he's talking to?"

"Why?"

"He has contacts with Cuba and there's a shipment coming in next week. I heard he's selling arms outside of the agreement and if I find out it's true, he's in a shit load of trouble."

"I'll keep my eyes open."

"Thanks, bro."

For a moment there's silence before Leo sighs. *"I should go. Stay safe, brother."*

"You too and call me when you have eyes on that will."

"Consider it done."

He cuts the call and for a moment I stare into the glass and wish things had been different. When Diana played us off against one another, the person who suffered the most was our sister Eliza. We were so caught up in our own anger that we left without a backward glance, leaving her to deal with Mario and Diana on her own. No wonder she ran and look where that got her. Blown to pieces along with my father. A cruel life extinguished alongside an innocent one.

I pour myself another whiskey to dull the guilt I constantly feel every day that I never protected her. Maybe that's why I'm so protective of Abi. If I couldn't save Eliza, I'm damn well saving my wife.

CHAPTER 18

ABIGAIL

The dresses Matteo had sent over were exquisite. I'm in love with a midnight blue satin gown that hangs off the shoulder, cinched in at the waist with a huge skirt that trails behind me. However, the red dress is exceptional, and I shiver with delight when I pull on the scraps of red lingerie and step into the dress. The red silk molding my curves and the huge split to my thigh makes me feel sexy and promiscuous.

Then again, since meeting Matteo, I have made the word promiscuous mine in every way. If I'm not fucking him, I'm thinking about it, and I wonder how this happened. It all began in his office at his club, watching my current boyfriend engaging in acts I never believed possible. It intrigued me, but not half as much as the man who made it happen.

He is like a dark flame that burns on pure evil. Raw, desirable and wicked, everything a respectable girl should sprint away from. Not me. I run toward it at speed because he makes me feel so alive when he is bringing me to my knees.

I pile my hair on top of my head and apply my make-up with care and precision. I'm excited for tonight, not because of the charity gala. Those events bore the pants off me quicker than Matteo can rip them off but being on the arm of a man like Matteo Ortega is breath-taking in its wickedness. My mom will hate the photos circulating among her friends when she sees his hand in mine. She will blow a fuse when news of our nuptials leaks to her friends and she will demand my return immediately when he flouts our relationship in her face as we mingle with known associates of theirs, causing me to wonder once again why she agreed to it in the first place.

With a shiver of excitement and a spray of the expensive perfume that arrived with the delivery, I am ready to face my future with all guns blazing. Matteo *is* my future; I can feel it almost as much as the excitement that's driving my heart to pound like a piston at full throttle. This is the best experience of my life, and I don't want to waste a second of it.

I head off to meet him and my mouth waters when I find him standing by the window in the living room, gazing out across the skyline.

He looks so dangerous dressed all in black, his shirt unbuttoned low enough to reveal that insane body scripted with dark intent. His belt buckle gleams as it catches the light and I pray I discover what his idea of punishment is when we return. His dark hair is styled short but long enough to feel luxurious, as it drifts through my fingers and the scuff on his jaw shows he doesn't give a fuck for appearances.

Most of the men I know are clean shaven and dressed in the best tailor-made suits. Matteo is no different but sticks two fingers up at convention and does what the fuck he likes. I admire him for that, and as I head into the room, he fixes that lustful gaze on me as I walk slowly toward him, making sure to expose the bare leg that peers out from the slit in my dress. The neckline is low and holds my assets in place like a lustful lover, and I have never felt as sexy in my life as I do now.

Evidently Matteo thinks so too because his tortured groan makes me smile and my eyes flash with victory as he moves to my side in two steps and slides his arm around my waist, caressing my ass with an ownership that makes me crumble.

He dips his lips to my ear and whispers, "You are beautiful, princess."

"Thank you." My breath hitches as he steps back and reaches inside his jacket and pulls out a velvet-covered box.

"Turn around."

My heart flutters as his fingers slide around my neck and fasten a diamond choker that nestles against my skin like a branding iron.

He whispers close to my ear, "Now everyone will know you are mine."

He spins me around, and the possession flashing in his eyes makes me almost pant with desire, and he says in his dark voice, "This collar tells everyone you are mine."

"It's only a necklace." I finger it reverently, and he laughs softly. "To anybody who doesn't realize its purpose."

I'm confused, and he reaches out and presses his thumb against my lower lip, whispering huskily, "Anybody who knows how domination works will understand you are mine. They can look but not touch, and that gives you more protection because of what you're wearing."

"I never knew."

I sense my eyes shining because who wouldn't want to be marked by a man like Matteo and I shiver as he brushes his lips against mine and whispers, "I'm going to fuck you in that dress, and I haven't decided where yet."

His words light a trail of desire inside me at the mere promise of what he has in mind, and he laughs softly. "Do you like that, princess? Wondering where it will be? The car perhaps, possibly the venue itself. In the street, in the alley like a common whore, or back here in my dungeon. I wonder what it will be?"

Images of every place crash through my mind and I'm incredibly turned on as he reaches for my hand.

"Business first." He winks, causing me to cross my legs because I would gladly sacrifice an evening in public for five more minutes on the terrace with him.

* * *

As expected, we don't travel lightly, and the usual three cars are waiting in the underground car park.

Cesare makes certain we are safely in the middle before jumping into the one in front, several of his soldiers taking the one behind us. As the cars begin to move, I shake my head. "Is this really necessary? It's all a little staged if you ask me."

He shrugs. "It serves many purposes. A warning, protection and business."

"Business?" I'm confused, and he nods, running his arm along the back of the seat and pulling me against him.

"My business is being better than everyone else, so they don't challenge me. The Ortega empire has existed over several generations, and it hasn't come easily. We have reached a place where we are respected and safe to a degree, but there is always a manipulative bastard waiting to snatch our crown."

"Your stepmother." I shiver when I think of her and Mario and Matteo nods. "They will be at the gala tonight. I thought I should warn you."

I stiffen as my head spins with this information.

He growls, "Tonight they will discover you are mine. It will be interesting to watch their reaction to that."

My earlier euphoria is in tatters as I contemplate meeting the gruesome twosome again, and then he makes it worse by saying casually, "Jefferson will also be there."

"What?" I stare at him in shock, and he nods, obviously

amused at something. "It will be good to catch up with old friends, won't it, princess?"

"If you say so." I stiffen at the thought of my past invading my present making me retreat into myself.

I'm surprised when a strong hand grips my chin and turns me to face two dark flashing eyes, the danger in them causing me to swallow hard.

"You are my wife, Abigail, and I expect you to act like it. Be proud of who you are and take no shit. You are Abigail Ortega now and not the pretty princess who does as mommy tells her. The apple of her daddy's eye and a girl with no brain. You are a mafia bride and I expect you to own it. Make me proud to call you mine and take no shit from anyone."

His words strike me deep because he's right. I am no longer a Kensington. I'm an Ortega now and with a man like him beside me, nothing can ever touch me again.

I nod as his eyes flash deep into my soul and I say huskily, "I won't let you down."

He strokes my face in a surprisingly gentle move and whispers, "I'm proud to call you my wife, Abi. I want you to know that."

The storm in his eyes turns me on and I surprise myself when I fix him with a mischievous smile and reach for his belt.

He is shocked when I unbuckle it and unzip his pants, dropping my head to his lap as I slide him into my mouth.

His tortured groan makes me smile as I take him in, loving how he thrusts in deep. Then I bite down gently, causing him to growl, "Fuck me!"

I suck him hard and fast, causing him to shoot deep down my throat. His heavy breathing telling me he is so turned on and as I swallow his salty cum, I love knowing it's marking me inside. Then, with a wicked grin, I zip up his pants and fasten his belt, saying softly, "Remember who owns this, too. When those women fling their inviting eyes in your direction, know you belong to me. It's my body responsible for giving you pleasure and mine alone."

My eyes flash as I stare at him with a new power inside me and I love how his smile lights his handsome face.

Then he pulls me close and whispers darkly, "So you believe you are strong enough to take the whole of me?"

He licks the side of my face and bites down hard on my lower lip. The flash of pain it creates turns me on and as I hitch my breath, his fingers slide around my neck, restricting my breathing, causing me to struggle for air and he growls, "One thing you should learn, princess, nobody dominates me, so if you think I'm happy about your little stunt back there, think again. You've just earned yourself a punishment for taking without permission."

He releases me, and I slump back in my seat with a small smile on my face. How does he know me so well already? That turned me on to the point of explosion and now I'm going to have to deal with the anticipation for the rest of the evening.

He shifts away and leaves me shivering with desire for the rest of the journey, completely ignoring me as he taps on his phone. Far from annoying me, though, it's making me want him even more and this gala can't end soon enough for me.

CHAPTER 19

MATTEO

Fuck me, that was the best blow job I ever had. When Abigail took control of the situation, it made me mad. Nobody takes control of me and yet it was so hot, I loved every second of it. My cruel treatment of her afterward merely stoked the flames even higher and I am impatient to bring this evening to a close because she has earned a visit to my dungeon for her sins.

The fact she is craving that more than anything makes me smile because my little rich girl has some incredibly carnal urges, and I can't wait to plunge her over the edge of the darkest cliff and dive after her.

We reach Madison Square Garden and I see the line of limos waiting to deposit their owners onto the red carpet and have a sense of pride knowing I will be stepping out with Abigail. Not my usual date, usually a whore or the daughter of a man who owes me a favor. This time I will walk beside my wife and once again I congratulate myself on a plan well executed.

Abigail is excited, I can tell as she fidgets on the seat beside me, a mess of lust, excitement, and fear. I know she is dreading seeing Jefferson and fears seeing Mario and Diana. She has no reason to fear it though because of who holds her hand.

We reach the red carpet and one of my soldiers opens the door, Cesare standing to his left, watching us exit with amusement in his eyes. I know he's loving every second of this. Seeing me with a respectable woman is unusual and seeing me with a wife is astonishing.

Flashbulbs light our way and as I reach for Abigail's hand, it curls into mine, causing a surge of protective desire to race through my body.

I am conscious of how she works the red carpet like a pro. Standing confident and proud, her dazzling smile lighting up the lens of many hardened paparazzi.

They call her name, and she turns and flashes them a rewarding smile and I set my own expression to bastard as I glare at anyone who even looks in her direction. Beauty and the Beast is a description that could have been written with us in mind because I am standing by her side baring my teeth and sharpening my claws, prepared to go for the jugular if anyone steps out of line.

Somehow, we make it inside and as we join the throng of guests, Abi grips my hand tightly.

We make our way into the great hall and the music that greets us is at odds with the danger lurking in every shadow.

As we help ourselves to two glasses of champagne, a seductive voice brushes against my left ear.

"You naughty boy."

It's as if she holds a serrated knife sliding down my skin and I turn and stare fiercely at Demelza Gregory, looking like Morticia Addams in a floor length, figure hugging black gown, her long dark hair like a sheet of ebony flowing down her back.

Her red painted lips are pursed seductively in my direction and her dismissive gaze falls on my hand, clasping Abigail's.

"Is there something you want to tell me, darling?" She purrs, her voice with an edge of steel that promises to cut me deep.

"Demelza, meet my wife, Abigail." I waste no words on pleasantries and love how the storm in her eyes reveals her inner thoughts in a flash.

"Your wife." She spits the last word and stares at Abigail as if she's a bad smell.

I feel my temper rising, but then Abigail says lightly, "Yes, Mrs. Ortega, and you are...?"

Demelza's eyes narrow. "His girlfriend."

The fact it's a bare faced lie has me reacting in a second, but Abigail is faster, and she says imperiously, "Then I win darling, so run along and lick your wounds. He's off the market, so maybe you should focus your attention on someone who's willing for a change."

She tugs on my hand, and ordinarily I would be angry at her show of dominance, but for some reason it makes me smile. As we walk away, she whispers, "If you don't like the monster you created, you only have yourself to blame, Mr. Ortega."

She smirks and my hand itches to connect with her shapely ass as she makes a mockery of my instructions, but then all other thoughts are banished immediately when a familiar face stops in front of us.

"Matty."

My heart takes a huge tumble as I stare into the beguiling eyes of the one woman who ever chipped away a piece of my black heart.

"Diana." I nod coolly, trying desperately to get my turbulent thoughts under control as she glances up at me from under her long dark lashes that hide the most astonishing blue eyes. Diana Corlietti has always been a fragile beauty that made me to want to protect. She stands before me like a vision in a white dress, her hair long and flowing down her back like a goddess.

Abigail's breath catches as she gasps, and I must have let my feelings show because I can sense her pain. Diana has always affected me and made me into a man I despise and seeing her now has brought it all flooding back as she stares at me with a mixture of hurt and desire mingling into an intoxicating cocktail. There was a time I would have craved hearing my name spill from her tempting lips. Ached to see those eyes fastened on me with that loving expression. Killed for one more night with her, one more luxurious decadent experience of forbidden love and broken promises.

However, the tide has turned because after my initial shock, the pain hits me like a tidal wave and washes away the rose-colored mist that latches onto my eyes when she's around.

Now I see her for what she always was, demented, twisted and cruel, forming a once beautiful girl into a woman who is ugly on the inside disguising what's on the outside.

"Stepmother." I cut her down with that one word, telling her I haven't forgiven or forgotten her betrayal and the tears well in her eyes as she whispers, "Please, can we talk?" She glances dismissively at Abigail and says with a tremble to her lips, "Alone."

"No." I dismiss her request with a cruelty that she deserves and tug Abigail along with me, creating distance between us.

Abigail is silent and I can tell she is shocked by my reaction, but I can't deal with that right now because it's as if our enemies are forming a line as the one person I hate more than my stepmother crosses our path, causing Abigail to squeeze my hand so hard I think she will break it.

"Mr. Ortega." Mario's slimy voice seeps into my blood and makes it boil on impact and I look eagerly at his reaction as he turns to my wife.

"Miss. Kensington." The expression on his face tells me everything I needed to know, because he can't disguise the yearning he has for the woman by my side. It's raw hunger,

ORTEGA MAFIA – THE CONSIGLIERE

perverted even, as he stares at her, almost salivating at the mouth. His cruel, beady eyes slide across her body, and he licks his wet lips as he reaches for her hand.

"Back off, Mario." I growl as I pull her behind me and then say with the utmost satisfaction. "And it's no longer, Miss. Kensington. Abigail is now Mrs. Ortega, my wife."

It's as if I've detonated a grenade, and it explodes in his face as he steps back and regards me through incensed, narrowed eyes. "Your wife!"

He almost can't form the words and I say smugly, "Yes, aren't you going to congratulate us?"

I am enjoying myself way too much, especially when he glances at Abigail and hisses, "Did he force you?"

The look of anger he is directing her way is interesting. Then she says in a tight voice, "Of course not. I love my husband and couldn't marry him fast enough."

I almost believe Mario is going to kill me now as he steps forward and hisses, "You don't know what you've done."

Abigail retreats a little at the fury on his face and I get between them, my soldiers moving to surround us. Abigail is shaking but nowhere near as much as Mario as he hisses, "You've just declared war, Matteo. Gather your troops because you don't know what you are facing."

The air darkens, the atmosphere oppressive and woven with sinister intent. I have never seen Mario lose his cool before. He usually walks around with a smug superiority and now that all falls away, revealing the demon inside.

Abi is afraid. I can almost touch her fear, and that causes the beast inside me to roar as I get in his face and snarl, "Then bring it on because you are a dead man walking."

I shove him away and my soldiers effectively position him out of our tight circle and clear a path through the astonished faces of the guests, who are suddenly aware of a storm about to break.

CHAPTER 20

ABIGAIL

Nothing prepared me for what happened. It was a vicious onslaught that appeared to go on for hours. First that woman who tried to stake a claim on my husband, then another who I fear more than anything from his reaction to her. It was obvious there's a history there that runs deep, and for the first time since I met him, I saw a little of his walls crumble. It leaves me with a hollowness inside. As if I'm second best somehow and if she had her way, she would take my place in a heartbeat and neither of them would look back.

Then there was Mario. That disgusting waste of skin and bone who chills me to the soul. I hated him on sight the first time I met him, and that opinion hasn't changed. He made my skin crawl and my eyes bleed because there was something sinister and deadly about the man who appears to have an agenda where I'm concerned.

Thank God Matteo is who he is and surrounds himself with menace because I doubt I could have got away from him if I was alone.

There is so much to process and yet I must maintain my

dignity because we are in public. To do a job and I must disguise my emotions.

Somehow, we end up on opposite sides of the room and as Matteo reaches for a glass of whiskey, I note it hardly even touches the sides, which shows how affected he is. Was it Mario or was it Diana? I have a sinking feeling it was her and I'm not sure of my emotions right now.

"I need to use the restroom."

I choose the only place I can go where privacy is guaranteed to go over what happened and bring my thoughts back in line. Matteo appears angry at that and snaps, "Can't you wait?"

"No." I pull my hand roughly from his and stare at him with a mixture of anger and pain, noting how the fury only intensifies in his eyes as he nods to Cesare.

"Stay with her and make sure nobody enters that restroom but Abigail."

Matteo turns away, leaving me feeling like a used dish rag.

I have gone from euphoric to desperate and want to sob my heart out because I'm fast realizing I am merely a pawn in a greater game that makes me feel used. Matteo doesn't want me, not really. He loves Diana. That was so obvious and is using me to get back at her. The other woman said she is his girlfriend. Why would she say that if it wasn't true and will he carry on with her when his use for me is over?

Suddenly, I feel like a fool. Everything comes at me and knocks the shine from my soul. He's using me. I'm only a distraction and what I felt earlier has been destroyed in a matter of minutes.

Cesare appears almost sympathetic as he escorts me to the restroom and I'm surprised when he says in a low voice, "Don't read too much into it."

"Into what?" I snap back, hating how harsh I sound, and he whispers, "He's reacting to the situation. Mr. Ortega has spent a lifetime hiding emotion and when he's hit hard in all directions, he uses aggression and anger as a defense. You are good for him, Mrs. Ortega, because you drag that from inside him and he hasn't figured out a way to use it yet. Don't judge him; he'll work it out."

We reach the restroom and I say coldly, "Maybe I don't want to hang around while he decides what he wants."

I'm surprised when his hand reaches out and prevents me from entering the restroom by holding onto the handle as he says darkly, "Don't do anything stupid. Mr. Ortega is your way out of a very bad situation and the only one you can trust."

I glare at his hand pointedly and say with a soft hiss, "Thank you for your concern, now if I may…" I nod toward the door and with a sigh, he steps back, allowing me inside.

As I head into the room, my heart bangs mercilessly inside me and I lean against the tiled wall, grateful to be alone to process my thoughts.

So many things happened so quickly I'm struggling to catch up. But I realize one thing, I am destroyed. I know that already because there's a dull ache inside me that's replaced my earlier euphoria. Above everything, it was Matteo's reaction to Diana that I can't shake, and I am weak with disappointment that he still holds feelings for that woman. She didn't even acknowledge me. It's as if I was invisible and they only had eyes for one another.

I'm so preoccupied I don't even register I'm not alone until a familiar voice whispers from a cubicle that I didn't know was occupied.

"Abi."

I spin around and my eyes fill with happy tears when I spy my best friend Clarice staring at me in disbelief.

"What's happened to you?"

In two steps she is by my side, and I fall into her welcome arms and sob on her designer gown, my mascara streaking the fabric.

"It's a mess."

"What is?" She strokes my hair, and it's so good having someone with me who only has my interests at heart.

She tugs me down beside her on a bench under the window and whispers words of comfort.

"It's ok, you can tell me everything."

I don't even think twice, and the words spill out in a rush, tripping over themselves to be heard as I tell her everything that happened since my first meeting in Matteo's office.

When I finish, she whispers, "Oh honey, you poor thing." She strokes my hair and appears as upset as I am.

"What are you going to do?"

I lean back and wipe my eyes with a tissue, unconcerned with what a mess I must look like right now.

"I don't know. My mom will kill me because I've done something so bad she will never recover socially. Then there's Matteo. I'm his wife now and I'm not even sure he wants me."

"I can't believe it." She shakes her head in disbelief.

"It's a mess."

"You could say that?"

A loud knock makes us jump and Cesare growls through the door, "What's taking you so long?"

I sigh and stare at my friend with a dull resignation.

"I should go."

Clarice glances at the door and lowers her voice.

"I can help you escape them all if you like."

"How?"

There is no way we could even take two steps before Matteo's soldiers bring me back and Clarice nods toward the open window.

"We're on the ground floor. I'm guessing this leads to an alley. Why don't we give it a try?"

"And then what?"

She giggles with excitement. "We catch a cab and head for my father's apartment."

"Is he there?" I'm doubtful, because Clarice's father would be on the phone to mine the minute he set eyes on me.

"No, he's out of town and I came here for the weekend. I used his ticket to the gala to have some fun, which is a very good job, because now I can save you."

A second is all it takes for me to make my decision and I jump up and whisper, "Let's give it a try, at least."

As we jump onto the bench and bend over the sill, I can see she was right. There is a short drop, to an alley to the side of the building.

We waste no time and tumble headfirst through the window, trying to suppress the giggles that remind me of similar escapades in our past.

As we drop to the ground, she grasps my hand, and we tear off toward the rear of the building and quickly flag down a passing cab. The driver rolls his eyes as we spill giggling inside and huffs, "Where to, ladies?"

As Clarice rattles off the address, I sink back in my seat and close my eyes, my heart thumping with adrenalin as I struggle to come to terms with everything that's happened.

At least I got away, that's something at least and as the cab flies through the city, I take a moment's satisfaction imagining the anger on Matteo's face when he realizes his bird has flown the cage.

CHAPTER 21

MATTEO

"Where the fuck is she?"

I hiss as Cesare heads to my side alone and looking so worried I can tell something has happened.

As he fills me in, my anger increases and he's just lucky we're in public right now because I'm itching to empty my gun into his head.

"Search this fucking place." I growl at my soldiers before I storm to the restroom and fling open the door, the squeals of the women inside merely background noise to the rage that's making my head pound.

I race across to the open window and peer at the street outside and say through gritted teeth. "Cover the entire area. Crack open heads and waste souls until you discover where she went."

Cesare starts issuing instructions into his phone like bullets and I spin on my heels and head outside, passing through the crowds like a hot knife in butter, focusing on nothing but my need to find my wife.

As we hurry from the building, I race down the steps toward my waiting car and as the door closes behind me, something catches my attention from the corner of my eye that chills my blood.

Mario and Jefferson are deep in a discussion on the sidewalk and don't appear to have seen me. Almost immediately, Jefferson steps into a car that pulls up and Mario heads back up the steps toward the gala.

Cesare slides in beside me and I point to Jefferson's car.

"I never knew Jefferson Stevenson was familiar with Mario?"

Cesare seems confused. "What makes you say that?"

I fill him in, and he says thoughtfully, "I'll do some digging."

There is something happening I can't place; it's surrounding me like a storm waiting to break. Everything that happened tonight swirls around my mind, and I think of Abigail and why she felt the need to run. I'm not proud of my reaction to Diana, but surely, she wasn't threatened by that. Was it seeing Mario? Is there something I'm missing and there's more to it than she's letting on? Then there's Jefferson. Is he involved in this somehow and was he sent by her father to bring her home? Was it all one big trap they set to bring me down and Abi was the bait that tempted me?

My head hurts as every possible scenario runs through my mind, and I don't even trust my own instincts right now, so I reach for my phone and text my brothers.

MATTEO

> Find out what you can about Jefferson Stevenson and Mario Bachini. I saw them talking in shadows. There's something we're not seeing.

LEO

> I'm on it.

> **DOM**
>
> There's something you should know. Call me.

I waste no time and as soon as I hear his rough voice, I snarl. "What it is it?"

"There's an organization called The Dark Lords. Remember, they took Flora and Mario, and Diana were involved."

I remember the story and say roughly, "What's that got to do with Jefferson?"

"When we busted Flora out, we ripped some names from the bastards who thought it would spare their lives. Stevenson was among them. Judge Stevenson."

"And you think Mario and Jefferson are connected through this fucked up organization?"

"I'd be surprised if they weren't."

"So, what are you saying?"

"I'm saying not to trust any of the fuckers because this is twisted shit that gets people's hearts ripped out. My advice is to follow them, and they will lead you to your answer."

There's a brief silence and I hate the quiver in my voice when I say, "Abigail's gone."

"How?"

"Shit went down, and she escaped through the restroom window. We're searching for her now."

I'm surprised at the genuine concern in his voice as he says gruffly, *"Then find her and fast because if she's involved in that fucking dark lords shit, you may never see her again and your plan will be over before it's even begun. My advice is to keep tabs on Mario and Jefferson. They may know something."*

He sighs heavily and then surprises me by softening his gruff voice. *"Take care, brother. Call me if I can help."*

"Thanks man." I cut the call, hating the emotion surrounding me when I think of my brothers. Despite falling out, we only have each other's best interests at heart, showing the power of family. They will kill for me, and I would do the same and yet now I have something else to think about and the fear for my wife grows by the second causing me to snap, "Tell the driver to take us to Jared Kensington's penthouse. I'm guessing she's there."

Cesare taps on the window and issues the instructions and I sit back in my seat and glance out of the window, praying I'll catch a glimpse of red in the shadows.

It doesn't take us long before we reach the swanky apartment block where Jared has his penthouse and, as we spill onto the streets, Cesare presses a huge bundle of dollars into the doorman's hand and says darkly, "Jared Kensington."

The doorman nods and steps aside, whispering what we need in Cesare's ear.

We waste no time and crowd into the private elevator, and Cesare taps in the code that the doorman let slip.

Inside of two minutes we are stepping through the doors and as I flick on the light and it illuminates the billionaire's paradise, my heart sinks when I realize there's nobody home.

"Search the place."

Cesare instructs my soldiers and as they spill out in every direction, I wander over to the skyline and glance down at the city I rule through fear. Here I am king. The Ortega empire is a poison running through this corrupt city and if my wife is hiding on the streets, it won't be long before she's returned to me. However, I'm doubtful of that, just hoping she's pissed and will show up here at daddy's apartment, hopeful of licking her wounds in a familiar space, so I settle down to wait for her.

The soldiers return empty handed and Cesare takes the seat beside me and whispers, "Empty, but you may want to take a look in his den?"

"Why?" I'm standing immediately and he says in a low voice, "It appears he keeps his files here. There's a huge cabinet and on closer inspection, there are some names in there you may be interested in."

I waste no time and follow him and as he opens the door, the masculine smell of cigars and brandy remind me how much I need both right now.

Cesare switches on the light and I take a seat at Jared's huge walnut desk and as Cesare brings several files for my inspection, I can see he was right to bring it to my attention.

It makes for interesting reading and prompts me to conduct a search of my own and I'm rewarded when I discover the false bottom to his desk drawer and pull out a black leather folio that has a gold embossed script on the front.

D and L entwine around a dagger and Cesare peers over my shoulder as I open it.

As we leaf through the pages, snapping photos of everything in it, my dread turns to a real fear. What the fuck is going on?

Cesare whistles slowly. "This is serious shit."

"Bastards." I growl as my life plummets off the edge into a dark abyss below.

Now it's even more important to find my wife because, from the look of this shit, she doesn't have long.

CHAPTER 22

ABIGAIL

Clarice lets us into her father's apartment and says with a sigh. "Thank God, we made it."

"For now." I remind her because if I know one thing about Matteo Ortega, he will find us in the end and I may not like my punishment, despite craving one earlier.

She heads to the kitchen and flicks on the kettle.

"We could use something stronger, but a coffee would be good for now."

As I kick off my shoes, I hate how betrayed I am. It's as if Matteo clawed out my heart and set it on fire because sensing his need for that woman killed any happiness I had inside me stone dead.

I want to sob into a pillow and forget I ever met Matteo Ortega, but how can I? I married the bastard and now I'll have to face my parents and tell them I made a huge mistake.

It doesn't feel like a mistake, though. It still feels like the best decision of my life, especially when I remember how amazing it was when I was in his arms.

I love him.

ORTEGA MAFIA – THE CONSIGLIERE

That stuns me because when did this materialize into love? How can I love a man like that? Then again, how can I not?

Clarice thrusts a steaming mug of coffee toward me and says with a cheeky wink, "I know where the brandy is. Perhaps we can add some to make it go down better."

"You read my mind."

I watch as she heads to a cupboard and pulls out a bottle and tips some into my mug before doing the same to hers.

"To bastards." She raises her mug to mine and as I take a sip, I relish the burn as it slides down my throat.

"So, distract me, honey, and tell me about your love life."

I really need to escape from my reality right now, and she appears a little on edge when she stares at me with a guilty expression.

"I'm sorry, Abi, I should tell you something."

"What?" I'm a little confused by her expression and she sets her mug down on the table and paces across to the window.

"I was there with Jefferson."

"My Jefferson!" I stare at her in shock, and she turns and her eyes flash with guilt, telling me this a story I need to hear.

"When you left, he was so angry. I was there at brunch and watched you walk out with that man."

She shakes her head. "I got talking to Jefferson afterward, and he was so bitter. He told me there was no going back for the two of you and for some reason, something sparked between us."

"What do you mean?" I'm buying some time because it's obvious what she means as she whispers guiltily, "I'm sorry, honey, but I thought you were over. Well, Jefferson and I kind of hooked up, and this trip was to get away from Washington and have some fun."

"So, where is he now?" I jump to my feet because the last person I need to deal with now is him and then my skin crawls when a deep voice says roughly, "I'm right here."

I turn and see Jefferson leaning against the door, looking anything but happy to see me and I stare at him in shock before glancing back at Clarice, noting her heightened color, the guilt spreading across her face as she glances at him nervously.

"I should go." I stand and Jefferson laughs out loud.

"You are making a habit of running out on me."

He shakes his head and moves beside Clarice, taking her hand and kissing it, his eyes flashing as he stares at me with a hard glint in his eye.

"You did me a favor."

"How?"

My head is spinning, and he snaps, "The fact you married that bastard lets me off the hook."

"You know about that?" I'm shocked, and a lazy grin stretches across his face.

"Yes, and thank God was my response. Imagine being saddled with a frigid bitch for a wife, needing to get my kicks with whores because I married the ice queen."

I stare at them both, noting the embarrassment on Clarice's face as he runs his hand inside her dress and pulls her breast out. He bends down and sucks it into his mouth and I look away because what the fuck is he trying to prove?

Clarice is embarrassed. I can tell by the way she says quickly, "Jefferson, please, not…"

"Not now, darling. That wasn't what you said when you entertained my friends. When we took it in turns to fuck your greedy ass while they snorted cocaine off your tits."

Clarice bursts into tears as Jefferson rages on.

"You see, Abigail, your friend is a whore dressed in designer sin. She wanted what you had so badly she would do anything to wear my diamond on her finger and when I told her what the initiation involved, she was fully up for it."

"Why, Clarice?" I stare at her with compassion because how could she degrade herself for him and she says almost spitefully, "Because it was hard always being second best. Watching you grab the best guy with the most prospects. The girl who had everything handed to her while the rest of us struggled to keep up. You were always so cool and detached. Never sinking to our level and allowing your emotion out. Every guy in society wanted you and when you left with a gangster, I stepped into your position and loved every minute of it. You fell off your pedestal, and I climbed up in your place."

"You're deluding yourself."

I try to plead with her because, despite everything, she's always been the best friend I ever had.

"How?" She glares at me. "You're the one with the criminal husband and no hope of ever climbing back on your throne. If this is what it takes for a lifetime of privilege, sign me up. It's not so bad, anyway."

"He's using you to get at me!" I shout and Jefferson laughs out loud.

"Don't flatter yourself. You're soiled goods and I wouldn't marry you now, even if my father disinherited me."

"That's fine by me. I never wanted to marry you in the first place."

I'm beginning to feel nauseous, and the room starts spinning. As I sit on the couch, I glance at the mug on the table and, for some reason, I realize it was spiked. Clarice blurs out of focus and Jefferson says as if from a distance, "As it happens, you were never going to be my bride anyway. Your family has already given that honor to another, and he's here to take you home."

I don't hear anything else or register his words because I black out and blissful ignorance pushes away the nightmare.

CHAPTER 23

MATTEO

We leave one soldier to wait in case Abi heads back to her father's apartment and waste no time in heading back to my own penthouse. I have instructed my soldiers to sweep the city and leave no stone left unturned, because she must be here somewhere. I have a tail on Mario and am frantically trying to get news on Jefferson. More soldiers are turning his family's apartment as we speak. If any of them show their faces, we'll be smashing them in and the only thing that matters is bringing my wife home.

I don't sleep and use brandy to keep me awake as I pace my apartment waiting for news.

The darkness turns to light and in the early hours, there is still no news of where she is.

I can't eat and I chain smoke to calm my frayed nerves because something is telling me things are only going to get worse because of what I read in that sick and twisted file.

Mid-morning, I have a visitor and the fact I'm exhausted catches me in a moment's weakness and I allow Cesare to show my stepmother into the room.

When I see her hovering nervously in the doorway, I'm relieved to discover I feel nothing at all for her.

"What do you want?"

I'm curt and cruel, loving how she winces under my derogatory gaze.

"Please help me, Matty."

Her voice is soft, and quivers and she looks so pathetic it shocks me.

"Help you! Why the fuck should I?"

I growl, sitting back on the couch, regarding her with a hooded expression.

"I don't know who to ask."

"Then maybe you shouldn't have made so many enemies."

I take another slug of brandy and relish the burn as she edges a little closer.

"I've missed you, baby."

I glance up and laugh out loud. "Why don't I believe you?"

"You should."

She reaches my side and drops to her knees before me and stares deep into my eyes.

"I thought about you every day since you left."

"Tell that to someone who cares."

"I think you do." I recoil as she rests her hand on my knee and bats her long lashes up at me.

"I was in an impossible situation."

"Of your own making." I remind her and she shakes her head. "It was Mario. He is blackmailing me."

"So, deal with it."

"I fell in love with you, Matty, and he made me choose."

"Love." I bark out a laugh. "You love games, Diana. Manipulation, deceit and stripping a man of his soul. That's your game and you're good at it."

"Please, Matty, you must believe me. You're all I have."

"Correction, had. I don't give a fuck anymore and you know why…?"

I push her so she falls back on the rug.

"Because you ripped out my heart and ground it to dust under your shoe, so if you think it still beats inside me, you'll find nothing but emptiness."

Her wide, hurt eyes stare at me in pain and for some reason it hits me, despite doing everything in my power to remain blind to it. Diana always knew how to manipulate me, and it appears she hasn't forgotten that devastating skill.

"How can I prove it?"

"By telling me everything."

I change direction and decide the stakes are too high to waste this golden opportunity and she looks down, leaving me in no doubt it's disguising the triumph flaring in her eyes.

"I will."

She whispers as if it's the most difficult thing she has ever done, and I shrug.

"Go on then."

She shuffles closer and takes my hand, causing me to snatch it back immediately.

"Please, Matty, believe me. It's taken a lot of courage for me to come here and fall on my sword. I will do anything to make you trust me again. We were so good together and Mario threatened me when he saw how much I love you. He threatened to tell your father and have us both murdered by his soldiers. I did it to protect us both, and I will not apologize for that."

"And my brothers?" I snap. "Was it the same for them too?"

She shakes her head sadly. "Mario again. He made me seduce you all to anger your father so he would order you to leave, then he could take your place and become your father's successor. Neither of us realized how soon that would be, and

I'd hoped to have more time to get away from Mario and plead for your forgiveness."

She sighs. "I prayed that something would happen and circumstances would do it for me in a gun fight. But Mario is like a cockroach and lives through the fire."

She falters and whispers, "I'm afraid of him."

As she speaks, it takes me back to the time I was happiest. When Diana was the center of my world and it's as if we are right back in that moment.

"Diana". I see her standing at the window and note how fragile she looks as she leans against the glass, an air of sadness surrounding her.

She says in a muffled voice, "Please, I need to be alone."

Something makes me step inside, rather than away and I move a little closer, hearing her strangled cry as she whispers, "Please, Matteo, I need to be alone."

I ignore her wishes and draw to her side, spinning her around to face me, and the anger boils when I see the fresh bruise covering her eyes.

"Did he do this?"

Her lip quivers as she battles the tears and just nods, trying to look away.

"The bastard." I growl, knowing that is the extent of my sympathy. My father has always spoken with his fists and fresh bruises were something we expected on our own faces but not on a woman's. If anything, I'm surprised at that because women in our family are treated like queens all the time they have their uses.

I reach out and she winces as I touch the purple stain on her beautiful face and her lip trembles as she whispers, "Please help me, Matty."

She shivers against the breeze from the open window, and I can't help myself and pull her into my arms. Her head resting against my chest as she sobs quietly.

My arms instinctively hold her to protect because I'm not the monster my father wants me to be and as she wraps her arms around my waist and presses her cheek to my chest, a surge of desire hits me hard in the heart.

Diana was paraded in front of us as our father's new girlfriend and he made no secret of the fact he was ruining her soul. We watched while he behaved inappropriately in front of us and turned away when he treated her cruelly and dismissed her opinion on just about everything.

My hatred grew for my father as rapidly as my infatuation with the woman huddled in my arms and without thinking, I drop a light kiss on the top of her head, more as an act of comfort than anything else.

She pulls back and the tears in her eyes are mixed with a deep yearning and as her lips hover dangerously close to mine, I can't help but steal a taste. She kisses me back with a hunger that matches my own and as she pushes her hands inside my shirt, just the sensation of her fingers on my skin makes my heart leap.

They lower to my pants, and she frees my already hard cock and I hiss as she drops to her knees and takes it into that tempting mouth. She sucks and licks and I thrust forward hard, loving the thrill of anger mixed with desire.

Dragging her up, I kiss her long and hard and she pants, "Fuck me, Matty. I want it to be you."

I waste no time in dragging her across to the bed and pushing her back, inching her dress up and spreading her legs. I push aside her panties, ripping them in my haste and as I fasten my lips onto her swollen ones, I taste pure heaven. Her soft gasps and moans make me blinded by lust and as I suck her swollen clit into my mouth, her juices are the sweetest taste on my tongue.

She mews like a kitten and is every bit as sweet as I haul myself up and thrust deep inside, loving how her walls clench around my cock, holding it tenderly as I fuck her so hard, it surprises me nobody hears.

It's something that happened whenever we were alone, without fear of discovery. It became the sweetest secret in the world, as we enjoyed a torrid affair behind everyone's backs.

I really believed she loved me. She told me often enough, and there were many whispered promises and plans for our future. I would have given my life for Diana. I loved her with all my heart and knowing my father was enjoying everything I loved tore me apart inside.

The day I found Domenico fucking her against a tree in the garden will be forever imprinted on my brain. I turned away, sick at what I saw, hearing her say the same words to him that she endlessly said to me.

I retreated away from the situation and began watching her more closely. Then my fears were realized when I witnessed Leonardo deep inside her in the boathouse one day.

She was confused when I maintained my distance and sought me out one day and I was cruel and callous, telling her I didn't love her and never had. She was just one more fuck you to my father, and it had always been a revenge fuck. Even then she implored me and declared her love for me, which brings me back to the present as I watch her say it all over again.

However, like the last time, she has something I want. Information. Abigail's life depends on it and as the mist clears from my eyes, I realize Diana could be useful to me in getting what I want and it only takes a moment's indecision before I fix a smile on my face and say softly, "I'll help you."

CHAPTER 24

ABIGAIL

My world swims into focus and with it, the knowledge that I'm in deep shit and it's doubtful anyone can save me.

I wake in a huge soft bed, littered with silk and scatter cushions.

I am still wearing the red dress I went to the gala in and the room I'm in appears to be a hotel one.

With a start, I sit up and stare around the unfamiliar room and note the fancy furnishings. Gold furniture set against papered walls. Huge flower displays and beautiful lamps, the drapes at the window the heaviest damask and the carpet on the floor soft and luxurious.

I'm thankful to note that I'm alone and swing my legs to the side of the bed and attempt to stand.

My legs are wobbly, but I make it to the window and am surprised to see a landscaped lawn, apparently leading into oblivion.

It's obvious I'm no longer in Manhattan and I wonder where this is and as I try to regain my senses, I jump when the door opens and the voice from my nightmares slithers through my brain.

"You're awake at last."

I turn and shiver when I see Mario heading my way, shirtless and wearing a pair of silk pants that hang off his skinny body in the most unflattering way. He is barefoot and his hair is greased back as usual, his malevolent eyes flashing as he sets a tray of food down on the side.

"Where am I?" My voice falters as he stands and regards me with interest.

"You are home."

"This isn't my home." I say angrily, and he shrugs.

"It is now."

"Take me back to New York, to my husband." I say as imperiously as I can, and he just laughs and nods at the tray.

"Your marriage is currently being annulled. It pays to have friends in high places, and Judge Stevenson is presiding over it now."

"How dare you!" I scream and he just shrugs again and hands me a mug of coffee.

"Just so you're aware, darling, our marriage has been agreed since you were sixteen years old. When you visited my home, the deal was struck. You, in return for the business, my father put your father's way. How does it feel to be sold by your own flesh and blood?"

"You're lying." I snap in the vain hope I'm right, but even I realize he is speaking the truth. It all slots into place and I say desperately, "Then why did my parents tell me I was marrying Jefferson? You're a fool if you think I'll believe a single word from your disgusting lips."

I know I've gone too far when his eyes flash and his lip curls and he spits, "It was Jefferson or me. That was the choice. When our fathers made the deal, it was to that effect. If

Jefferson couldn't be persuaded to marry you, then I would happily step in."

"But he did." I say exasperated, and he nods.

"That was before your boyfriend threatened to ruin him. He knew there was no way out but to step aside and let a greater warrior take his place. Matteo is like a bug to me, and I will soon stamp on him. When the Ortega family is under my control, the first thing I'll do is kill Giovanni's three sons. It's inevitable because their father foolishly believed everything I told him and cut them out of his will, gifting me the title of don instead. It's all worked out rather well for me, in fact, and now you will take your rightful place by my side as my bride."

"I would rather die."

He merely smirks. "It's funny you say that because if you don't marry me, you will be sacrificed to the Dark Lords. It's your choice."

"The dark what?" My head is spinning and Mario grins with a wicked glint in his eye.

"I'll demonstrate that later. You see, my home also doubles as our headquarters, and tonight there will be a ritual. I'll show you what happens to those who incur our wrath. It will make you aware how trapped you are. You see..." he moves across and a wave of revulsion hits me as he tugs me toward him and wraps his arm around my waist. His breath is rancid as he whispers close against my mouth, "The only way you live is married to me. Your father knows the score. He sold his soul to the devil years ago. It's why he's so successful, but that comes at a price."

I attempt to turn my head away, but he grips my face hard and whispers, "Your billions are drenched in the blood of the people your father stepped on to bank it. The price for that is total allegiance to the cause and the Dark Lords own his soul and now yours. You are to marry me to give me respectability."

He traces a finger down my face, making me shiver. "With

you beside me, I will rise like a phoenix from the ashes of hell and take my place at your father's side. I will be powerful, rich and perfectly placed to ensure the organization prospers. Jefferson is on a similar path but must now marry another. Someone who can elevate him to the biggest position in the land."

"You're mad." I hiss and he pulls me roughly against him and laughs like a sadistic demon.

"Mad for you, baby. You're just lucky I haven't fucked you already. Make no mistake, I will. With or without your cooperation."

"You're disgusting. Let me go."

"Never in a million years, baby. You're mine to play with at will, and I like to play a lot."

He grabs my dress, and the sound of tearing fabric fills the room as he rips it from my body and groans. His hand holding my hair in a tight grip as he pushes his tongue in my mouth. I almost retch as he grabs my breast hard, causing a bolt of pain to shoot through my body and then he growls, "Did I tell you I'm a sadist, baby? I'll enjoy watching your skin turn to fire under my touch. Prepare yourself for the pain because you'll have to live with that. My preferred pleasure being the bullwhip while I hunt you from room to room."

He slaps me hard around the face and I fall to the ground, receiving a sharp kick in my stomach for my sins.

"Now listen up, baby, because I'll say this only once. Do everything I tell you like a good girl because I have a short fuse. When I tell you to do something, you never question it and after the ceremony tonight, I'm going to enjoy hunting you."

"What do you mean?" I spit some blood on the floor, and he laughs like a maniac.

"I have a basement that doubles as a playroom. It's a maze of tunnels that I will let you explore in a bid for freedom. There is one way out, the rest leads to dead ends and if I catch you, you will wish the dead part referred to you. So, eat your food and strip naked for me, before putting on this robe. You have one hour to prepare yourself for a ceremony that will change your life. Our wedding."

He directs another sharp kick at my ribcage and, as I double over in pain, I am relieved when the door clicks shut behind him, leaving me wondering how the hell I'm going to escape from this nightmare.

CHAPTER 25

MATTEO

Diana's smile lights up her pretty face and she can't disguise the victory flashing in her eyes.

"You will."

"What do you need?"

I keep my tone casual, but I am burning up inside. It's obvious I'm not dealing with a sane person and one false move could end badly for Abi.

She sits beside me and places her hand on my leg, and I want to push it away so badly. The thought of her touching me makes me shiver, and she obviously takes that as a good sign and whispers huskily, "Fuck me, Matty. I have been dreaming of you ever since you left."

Her fingers rest on my limp cock and, shifting, I say with a sigh, "Not until I rid your world of that cockroach Bachini."

She nods, apparently accepting my brush off, and she leans in and fastens her lips to mine, her tongue edging inside in an act I dreamed of many times since I left her.

Kissing Diana is like a Judas kiss because it's as if I'm betraying Abigail by just breathing the same air as Diana. That alone surprises me because when did I play the loyal lover?

Only once, with Diana and since she broke my heart, I have fucked women with no emotion at all.

I try so hard to drag my mind back to that time, but all I taste is revulsion as her lips rest against mine.

She moans and whispers, "I want you so badly. Fuck me now, right here."

Luckily, the door opens, making my exit easy, and I pull away from her as Cesare enters the room.

"Boss, I need a word."

I forgive Cesare unconditionally for allowing Abigail to escape, merely for separating that woman's lips from mine, and I jump up and say over my departing shoulder, "Wait here."

As soon as we leave the room, I exhale sharply. "Thank fuck for the interruption. I was struggling back there."

Cesare nods. "Anytime."

He says with a sigh. "The guys have come up with nothing. There's no trace of them. Not even Jefferson. It's as if they've disappeared off the face of the earth."

"Or into it." I growl, reminding him of the vermin we're dealing with.

Turning toward the door, I sigh heavily. "Then that woman is our only hope. Why do I think it's a trap?"

"Because you understand how her mind works, I guess."

"That's what I'm scared of."

I exhale sharply and say with frustration, "We're at a dead end. Diana is our only hope, but it may cost more than I'm willing to pay."

Cesare shrugs. "Then defer payment."

It makes me smile because he always has such simple answers for complicated problems and detaches emotion with an ease I thought I had until I met Abi.

"Don't leave me alone with that bitch. It's time to get my wife back."

I make my decision in a heartbeat and head back into the room, Cesare hot on my heels.

Diana looks up and smiles, something in her expression telling me she knows she has backed me into a corner, and I hate that she's right.

"Tell me where Mario is now?"

"So, you'll help me?" She flutters her lashes and I nod. "I will."

She plays with the fabric of her dress and smiles. "Mario has a house in Boston. He prefers it there because it's a fortress."

We don't interrupt and let her speak, and I note the devious glint in her eye that makes me wonder if it's due to him or me.

"He has taken your, um, visitor there."

Suddenly, she looks up and stares at me with an expression of pain and whispers, "You don't love her, do you, Matty?"

I can tell it's important to her that I don't, and love isn't something I've ever considered until now. In my heart, I think I do because it hurts so much knowing she's in danger and I may not be able to save her. I shouldn't care, I shouldn't give a fuck actually, but it's become the most important thing in my life to bring her home safely.

However, even I realize Diana would hate knowing that, so I growl, "Love is an emotion fabricated by fools. I loved once and look where it got me."

My answer appears to satisfy her because she believes she is the only woman I have ever loved, which gives her a certain power over me.

She nods and glances past me to Cesare and shakes her head. "Two such powerful men. I knew this was the perfect place to come for help. Mario is out of control and needs to be stopped."

"Then tell us his address and any security measures we need to be aware of."

"He is using the Ortega soldiers as his own personal army.

They surround him, but their loyalty lies with you and your brothers. Mario may believe he's in control, but one command from you would make them turn on him."

I still can't work out if this is a trap and tread carefully. "The house. Can you get us inside?"

"Of course."

She smiles. "I have access to everything. Mario trusts me and I would have done anything he asked. I always have, but he betrayed me."

Her eyes flash and a corner of her mask slips, revealing the bitter, cruel woman who lives inside an outer packaging of innocence and vulnerability.

It's obvious she has a burning hatred for Abigail, something that obviously never left her. I'm guessing this is the reason for her visit. Not out of concern for anything he's done to her, out of her love for a man who wants someone else, and now I understand. Mario has made the fundamental mistake of betraying Diana for another woman and that makes me feel a lot better because now I know she will do anything to get him back and wants me to remove the woman currently beside him, permanently.

* * *

It doesn't take us long and we are soon on my private jet heading to Boston. Diana sits for most of the flight, staring out of the window or answering Cesare's questions about the security measures and agreeing to our plan to get inside.

If anything, she appears excited, which shows how twisted she is. There is still something advising me to proceed with caution though and so I make certain to dash out a text to my brothers informing them of current developments.

When we land, a message flashes up from my brother Leonardo that doesn't make me feel any better.

> **LEO**
>
> Mario's house in Boston is an old mansion built in the seventies. The current plans on file show it's built over several floors and has been modified to include a basement. The plans reveal a series of tunnels that lead down to the lake. Aerial shots show a boat house where the tunnel ends. It could be the perfect way in, but you would need to deal with any cameras that could be hidden. You would either walk into an ambush or hold the element of surprise.

I forward it to Cesare, who studies it hard, a look of concentration on his face as another text comes through.

> **LEO**
>
> I did some more digging on The Dark Lords and intel suggests they are active in Boston. I'm guessing Mario has some powerful friends there, so be prepared for that. Domenico is digging for information and will send anything relevant. Stay safe, brother, we've got your back.

I send a brief message of thanks and lean back in my seat and regard Diana through doubting eyes. This is all too easy, which tells me she's playing us. Why would Diana offer Mario as a sacrifice? It doesn't make sense after everything they've been through.

According to Dom's woman, Flora, Diana is in love with Mario and has always been infatuated by him, so I decide to do a little more digging before we leave the aircraft.

"What is Mario's plan concerning Abigail?"

"He wants to marry her."

She fixes me with a direct look and what I see in her eyes disturbs me—a lot.

"He's too late for that." I say roughly and she throws her head back and laughs. "Then you're a fool for believing you can stop him."

I freeze inside as she grins, the hatred flashing from her baby blue eyes. "It was always going to happen one way or another."

"But she was engaged to Jefferson Stevenson."

I'm so confused and Diana shrugs. "That would never have gone ahead, you see..." She leans forward and hisses, "Mario was never going to allow that to happen. He didn't count on you stepping in and sweeping his bride down the aisle first, though. He wasn't prepared for that."

"So now he's lost." I test the water carefully and Diana shakes her head. "Mario never loses. Ask yourself why we were at that Gala? Why Jefferson was at that Gala and why your bride never left with you?" She grins. "Mario planned it all and now he has what he wanted all along."

The bitterness in her expression disturbs me more than I'd care to admit. It tells me she's unhappy about Mario's infatuation with Abigail and that makes me fear for Abi's life. Diana is an unstable element that is likely to explode at any moment and I'm just grateful I have her in my sights because at least there, I can keep an eye on her.

I lean forward and say darkly, "I'll ask you again. What is Mario plan for Abigail?"

"She will marry him or die. It's simple. Honor the agreement drawn up by their fathers or be sacrificed to the Dark Lords. She has no choice; she's screwed either way."

"Sacrificed." I peer across at Cesare, who looks concerned. "What is this shit?"

I remember Domenico telling us what Flora went through and knowing Abigail is facing the same torment fills me with pain.

"That's why I'm helping you." Diana says sadly.

"To save Abigail's life?" That doesn't ring true and I'm shocked when she says with a sigh and a slight shake of her head.

"To save mine."

CHAPTER 26

ABIGAIL

When the door opens one hour later, my nerves are all over the place. I thought long and hard about how to play this because I need to deal with my fear and keep my wits about me.

I have done as Mario asked and am standing naked with the dark hooded robe pulled around me; the hood covering my face, offering a kind of protection that I'm grateful for.

Two figures stand in the doorway, wearing identical robes to mine and my heart sinks when I see they are wearing devil masks. As they approach, I say fearfully, "Please, let me go."

They say nothing and merely take one arm each and clamp metal handcuffs on my wrists, fastening them behind my back.

I call out, "Stop, what are you doing? I'm cooperating, for fuck's sake."

Once again, they say nothing and just push me toward the door and walk beside me like demons on my shoulder.

We move down the carpeted hallway, and I strain to hear any sound, but it's eerily quiet.

It's obvious Mario enjoys the best that money can buy

because this place is a palace. Expensive art and deep pile carpets that smell new and there is nothing out of place in a house that doesn't appear to be lived in at all.

The hooded figures lead me to a door at the foot of the stairs and my heart beats frantically when they open it, revealing stone steps leading down to what I imagine is the basement.

Is this the hunt that Mario promised me? Will they set me free to run for my life or is there something else?

They push me into a room that is shrouded in darkness, the cool breeze whistling through the stone walls chilling my blood. My feet hurt as I walk on rough ground and it's obvious, unlike the rooms above, this was designed for cold comfort instead.

We make our way into a huge room that makes me want to turn and run because, set in the middle, on a pedestal of sorts, is a stone altar. It is surrounded by candles that burn fiercely, casting the room in the fires of hell.

I glance nervously around and note several hooded figures standing around the altar, each holding a candle and then one steps forward as the two men guarding me step back.

My heart almost gives out on me as the figure removes his hood and I see the same devil mask covering his or her face. My heart thumps as I move back straight into the figures that are guarding me from behind.

The devil reaches out and pulls me close and, leaning down, whispers, "You make a beautiful bride, darling."

I shiver with revulsion at the sound of that voice, knowing immediately the identity of the sick and twisted bastard standing before me.

His voice slides over me like acid rain, burning as it causes irreversible damage.

"You have a choice. Marry me or die. What is it?"

"Kill me now, you bastard."

I spit in his face and am rewarded with a sharp slap around the head, momentarily blinding me and then as the fog clears, he spins me around and hisses, "Then maybe this will change your mind."

I stand bound and restrained, watching something that causes me so much pain I think I'm about to pass out when Clarice is pulled struggling and screaming into the room, naked and shackled just like I am. She has no robe to cover her modesty, and the fear in her eyes is palpable as she cries, "Please, let me go. I did what you asked."

I watch in horror as she is forced down on the stone altar by two hooded figures and shackled to it with metal cuffs.

Mario laughs softly beside me and whispers, "You'll enjoy this. She betrayed you, darling. She brought you to me knowing my plans for you. She was a fool."

"Why?"

The tears pour down my face as he shrugs. "She thought she could earn her position as Jefferson's wife. All it would take was an initiation of sorts to prove her loyalty. We used her and now we will use her again to change your mind."

"Why are you doing this?"

I sob and he laughs like a demon beside me. "Because I always get what I want, and I want it all. When facing death, people make interesting choices and I'm relying on your compassion to agree to my demands."

He grips my face hard and forces me to look at Clarice, screaming and sobbing as she is secured to the altar and he hisses, "Watch. This is the good part."

The hooded figures raise their candles and move around the altar. They begin a weird humming as they circle the screaming woman, dripping candle wax onto her naked skin, her screams echoing all around us.

"First, they torture her." Mario says with glee. "Burn her

skin and brand her with a hot poker. Have you ever inhaled the aroma of burning flesh, my beauty? It's exhilarating."

As if to prove his point, I stare in horror as one of the figures produces a burning hot poker and presses it hard against her left breast.

"Please, stop." I sob as Clarice's agonized scream pleads for mercy and Mario says roughly, "So you agree to my demands. Marry me and become my wife, 'til death us do part."

I watch a hooded figure step forward and thrust inside her, pumping furiously as he takes her against her will and I shout, "Enough, please let her go. I'll do it."

Mario's low laugh fills me with dread as he says in a loud voice, "Cease the ceremony."

The figures fall back and then turn to face us, still in a circle but facing outward instead. I note they are wearing the same mask and shiver inside. Who are they?

Clarice is sobbing and my voice breaks as I say, "Please release her. Let her leave and I'll marry you."

Mario raises his hand, and two hooded figures turn and release my friend and drag her away.

"How do I know you'll let her go? I won't marry you until I know she's safe."

Mario shakes his head, almost with disappointment, and growls, "You speak as if you have a choice, darling. You don't."

He steps forward and lowers my hood and delivers a fresh blow across my face, hissing, "I will beat you into submission every time you speak out of turn."

He stares at me through crazed eyes and almost screams, "Everybody leave. Return in one hour's time for the marriage ceremony."

As they file silently away. it chills me to the bone to be left alone with this maniac and when he produces a bullwhip from inside his robe, my knees almost give out on me at the sadistic glint in his eye.

"But first we'll have some fun. This is your chance to escape. You have a head start of fifteen minutes. There is one way out of the tunnels and the rest lead to eternal damnation. When I find you, I torture you, and when I've whipped you to the point of oblivion, you will give your soul to me for eternity."

He steps back and pulls a lever on the wall, and I stare in astonishment as a trap door opens and I note stone steps leading down to a cold looking pit.

"Off you go, darling. I'll see you soon."

He pushes me roughly and I fall into the pit and as the trap door slams above my head, I know I'm in the biggest trouble of my life.

CHAPTER 27

MATTEO

We reach the house, and I can tell why Mario chose it. It's in the middle of nowhere and anyone could watch our approach for miles.

Once again, I sense it's a trap and yet this time Diana isn't going to get away with using me.

I keep her close and say darkly, "What's your plan to get us inside?"

She laughs softly. "Wait and see."

"I don't trust you." I state the obvious and she turns and holds her palm flat against my face and appears hurt.

"I suppose I deserve your mistrust, Matty, but this time I'm telling the truth. I want you to get Abigail away from Mario and I will do whatever it takes."

The penny drops as I learn the real reason behind her request because Mario is the only person who matters in Diana's life, even more than her own. It's obvious she hates the idea of him marrying another woman and now I know what we're dealing with, I can mentally prepare for that.

We will be safe all the time Mario has Abi, but then the gloves are off. It's apparent Abi's life is in danger and it's not from the man holding her against her will. It's Diana. I'm guessing she will take her moment to strike, and a stray bullet, or a quick slice of the knife, will be all it takes to rid her of her nemesis.

She directs the driver to the front of the property and as we stop at the gates, she rolls the window down and says to the guard on duty, "Diana Ortega. Let us pass."

He peers inside the car and when he sees me beside her, he takes a second look.

"Mr. Ortega." He almost salutes, and the relief on his face surprises me a little.

He opens the gates and Diana whispers, "I told you. Their allegiance is to your family, not Mario, despite what he thinks.

"Do you really expect me to believe it will be this easy?"

I stare at her hard, and she shakes her head and almost looks contrite.

"I've hurt you, Matty. I accept that and I'm sorry. I was blinded by lust for Mario. He could do no wrong and he was everything I wanted. However, he showed me a side I am no longer comfortable with, and I want to make things right. For you, for your family and, well, for us?"

She blinks and bats her long lashes and I almost believe every word—almost. However, I've been here before and paid the price and I'm not about to make the same mistake twice.

"Tell me where we'll find Mario?"

I revert to business and ignore her pleading traitorous eyes and she says sadly, "In the basement. You will have the element of surprise because he won't believe for one second that you know where he is."

"The basement?"

She shrugs. "It's where the ritual is carried out."

"What fucking ritual?"

Diana sighs and appears angry as she hisses, "The Dark Lords. Mario has built a replica altar in his basement. He uses his staff to act as fellow lords and enjoys carrying out false ceremonies. It's why I came to you. He's out of control and is bringing unnecessary heat on the organization."

"You seem to know a lot about that." I stare at her hard and she shifts a little on her seat.

"I'm aware of how it works, but Mario has overstepped the mark in every way. He must be stopped before he brings the organization down."

Cesare is taking it all in and we share a look, both of us doubting every word that spills from her lying lips, but I don't have time for questions, it's actions Abigail needs now, so as I take out my gun and make it ready, Cesare does the same.

If we are about to face a gun fight with our own soldiers, we won't go down without a fight.

The car stops at the main entrance and Diana wastes no time in being the first one out, whispering, "I need to go ahead to clear your way."

I'm hot on her heels because I'm not letting the traitorous bitch out of my sight and as we head through the door, I'm amazed that the soldiers stand back and bow their heads.

It's all a little eerie and as Cesare organizes our troops, I watch as Diana's hand hovers over the door at the foot of the staircase. She turns and places her finger on her lips and opens it before pointing down some stone steps.

She heads through the door and as we crowd behind her, she whispers, "Listen."

We strain to understand what she's heard, but all I register is our own frantic breathing and I hate the worried stare she throws me as she says urgently, "We could be too late."

That's all it takes for me to push past her into a huge room that makes my skin crawl. It's creepy as fuck and I stare around me in surprise when I notice a stone altar set in the middle of the room with metal cuffs dangling over the edge.

"What is this?" I hiss and Diana replies, "It's the ceremonial room. The Dark Lords hold their ceremonies in one exactly the same and I told you Mario took it a step too far."

She nods toward the center of the room where I regard a massive open trap door that appears to lead into oblivion.

"Mario will be down in the tunnels, probably hunting your wife."

"Do you really expect me to believe—"

Suddenly, a sound like a gunshot makes its way from out of the pit and I hear the sadistic cackle of a madman. "Keep running, baby. Daddy's coming for you."

Diana looks so angry it stuns me for a moment and she says urgently, "Hurry, he's after her and when he catches her, he's going to hurt her bad."

Another crack of the whip follows, and I say to Cesare, "Stay here with some soldiers and make sure she goes nowhere. The rest follow me and if you see that fucker Mario, shoot to kill."

As I prepare to jump, Diana says urgently, "Be careful, Matty. They will both be dressed the same. It could be either one of them you see."

I heed her warning as I jump head first into hell, my soldiers not far behind me.

CHAPTER 28

ABIGAIL

I am so frightened. Cold, fearful and afraid for my life and it's so dark I have no idea where I'm going. I could be running around in circles for all I know, and yet the fear of what's behind me spurs me on.

My feet are freezing and hurt like hell. The floor is littered with sharp stones, which is probably why Mario wanted me to be naked under the robe. However, I would walk over hot coals to escape from him and if I stand any chance at all of survival, I need to be calm about this. For a moment, I stop and listen and hear nothing at all, and decide to feel my way in the hope I find a light switch at least.

I have nothing but my senses to guide me and as I edge along the wall, I pray that I find something to help me. Surely, there will be some form of light to guide me, a sliver through the stone wall, perhaps.

I choke back the tears when I think of how happy I was with Matteo. I never expected that. To fall in love so quickly and so hopelessly. But I ran from him because he loves another. It was obvious he was affected when the woman herself stood before him. I am just collateral to all the men in my life. My father almost gifted me to Jefferson and then offered no argument sending me off with Matteo. Then I learned that the substitute was Mario, and everything began to slot into place. My best friend betrayed me and yet her reward was so cruel I had to save her. Two wrongs don't make a right and I refuse to have that on my conscience.

Suddenly, the sound of a whip cracking is behind me and I almost scream in terror as I sense him closing in on me. His voice sounds far away, but it reaches me all the same and the chilling voice of a man I never want to see again drives fear into my heart.

"I can smell your fear, wife. You're so close I can hear your terrified panting."

There's another crack of the whip and then a manic laugh, followed by a low growl. "I'm going to cut you open until you beg for forgiveness. I will watch your blood run like a river of your stolen virginity because you never chose me. You married another man, and you must be punished for that. My wife is a whore, and I will treat you like one. Be prepared for a lifetime of pain because I'm an unforgiving master."

My sobs catch in my throat as I move faster, using the walls as a guide as I run from the madman chasing me.

My heart is thumping so hard I hope it doesn't give me away to the hunter behind me.

I want to scream so badly, but any sound at all will help him, not me and so I move as swiftly as I can in total darkness, feeling my way over rough terrain.

I sense him gaining ground and it's as if the air is choking me, the sound of the whip ever closer. His voice is getting louder, nearer, as he shouts in a voice drenched with sinister intent.

"You'll love being my slave, Abigail. Your father will have no choice now and will watch the light die in your eyes as I kill you inside. He will regret the minute he allowed you to escape with another man."

I try to move faster, but he appears to be gaining on me and his cruel laugh makes me shiver. "Jefferson was a safety net. A get out of hell free card, but he is weak and a fool. He is no match for me and will never rise to the same heights of power I will with you by my side. We'll be invincible, darling. Nobody can stop us, and you get the added bonus of being controlled by me. You will have my full attention and I'll enjoy every cruel second of it."

He is so close and I sense he's gaining on me now and a red glow lights up the space behind me, telling me he has help in navigating the darkness. It makes me angry because of course he would cheat. I was never going to win, and I move faster, my foot catching on a sharp stone, causing me to hiss with pain.

His voice slithers over my soul as I hear his heavy breathing and this time the crack of the whip is so close, I almost feel the air it disturbs.

I try to increase my pace, but I reach a wall and my heart lurches when I realize I've hit a dead end. There's no way out. I've walked straight into his trap and as the light gets closer, I pull the robe tighter around me in the vain hope it will protect me in the shadows. However, just when I think it's over, the wall shifts behind me and I tumble backward, then a firm hand presses against my mouth and I am pushed to the side.

I have no time to react before a soft voice whispers, "Come, we don't have long."

I can tell it's a woman's voice. Soft, sweet and calming and as I open my eyes and stare up at the figure above me, I notice they are shrouded in the same black cloak I am wearing.

"Quickly." Her voice is urgent, and I jump when I hear a growl from the other side of the wall.

"I know you're here, Abigail. Come to daddy."

The sound of the whip is close to my ear, and the woman pulls me up and sets off at a pace, and I struggle to keep up.

Thankfully, Mario's voice is getting fainter and as we run down a similar tunnel, I wonder who my savior is.

There's no telling at all as I race after the black figure, who appears to know exactly where she's going.

My breath is hot and heavy as I follow my unknown rescuer and as we reach the end of a dark tunnel, she stops, and another door opens. She pulls me through it onto a wooden staircase and as she closes the door behind her, she whispers, "We need to be careful; anybody could be at the top."

I have no time to discover who she is as she starts taking the stairs two at a time, my only thought is that her feet are bare like mine.

We reach the top of the staircase, and I am out of breath but exhilarated to have created distance between me and Mario. and as she reaches another door, she says in a whisper, "Prepare yourself for anything."

"Wait." I place my hand on her arm and she turns, the light revealing her face for the first time. She's a pretty woman, but there is raw pain in her eyes. It's as if she's lived a thousand nightmares and can't shake the demons they created and yet she smiles sadly and says with a sigh, "I hope you make it."

"What do you mean?"

She shakes her head and places her finger on her lips.

"Quiet. We need to tread with caution."

As she inches the door open, a shaft of light nudges through the crack and I swear my heart is racing double quick time.

As we edge inside the room, my heart tumbles because it appears I am right back where I started. The gruesome chamber reveals itself and strikes so much fear inside me, I may not survive the heart attack that appears imminent and as we enter, several pairs of eyes settle on us as the men in black turn and stare at us with astonishment.

I almost stumble when I see a familiar face and as Cesare starts running toward us, I watch with the greatest sense of relief of my life. In fact, all hell breaks loose as the soldiers turn and create a ring of steel surrounding us, but the biggest shock of all is that it's not me they are looking at.

"Stephanie."

Cesare's voice breaks as he gazes in disbelief at the angel who rescued me, and her sharp intake of breath reveals she is as surprised as I am.

"Cesare." Her voice falters and the tears aren't far away as she falls into his arms and huge sobs wrack through her body as he holds her tenderly.

Along with the soldiers, I stare at the scene in amazement, not really understanding what's happening right now and as Matteo's loyal soldier holds the woman he lost, so tenderly in his arms, I note the raw emotion on his face as he holds on tight as if he will never let her go.

CHAPTER 29

MATTEO

This place is creepy as fuck and as we silently pour into the tunnels, I instruct my men in a hoarse whisper to spread out and use their phones as a torch. To keep their guns ready and only when they are certain it's Mario, to shoot the fucker dead.

Two soldiers stay with me as we weave our way with deadly intent and as we move silently through the dark, damp tunnel, I have a real fear that we'll be too late.

It's an eternity before I hear a sound like a gunshot, and I still, my men stopping abruptly behind me. Then I hear the chilling voice of a walking corpse.

"Jefferson was a safety net. A get out of hell free card, but he is weak and a fool. He is no match for me and will never rise to the same heights of power I will with you by my side. We will be invincible, darling. Nobody can stop us, and you get the bonus of being controlled by me. You will have my full attention and I will enjoy every cruel second of it."

The red mist covers my eyes, and my blood boils as I surge forward, desperate to tear the fucker apart with my bare hands.

His voice edges out of the darkness. "I know you're here,

Abigail. Come to daddy."

I see a light in front of me and a cruel voice says darkly, "What do we have here? Visitors?"

We stop short and then the man himself comes out of the darkness and before I register what's happening, my gun is snatched from my grip with the flick of a whip.

Before I can react, he catches the soldier behind me and his cry of pain is accompanied by a gunshot as he fires his gun, the bullet way off target as it embeds itself into the wall.

My other soldier reacts, but a shot brings him down as Mario uses my gun on my own man and without thinking, I grab the gun from my one remaining soldier and hold it in front of me and fire at will.

I almost think I've found my mark when silence greets me and then a low laugh wafts down the tunnel toward me as Mario says with a wicked laugh, "Missed."

Then the whip catches my hand, causing the gun to fall from my grip and another sharp sting catches the side of my face. With a roar, I fall deeper into the tunnel, and I see his hooded body not far out of reach and as he raises his hand to have another go with the whip, I dive for his feet and pull them out from under him.

His painful grunt makes me smile as I rain blows down on his head and body with blind fury. Then, grabbing his whip, I wrap it around his scrawny neck and pull it tight, the sound of him choking music to my ears.

Footsteps come up fast behind me and my soldier says gruffly, "Let me help."

He grabs Mario in a headlock as I punch his face into oblivion and only when his body goes limp do I lean back on my heels and take a deep breath.

My thoughts turn to Abigail, who is still in this pit of hell, and I call out. "Abi, it's Matteo. Come out princess, we've got him."

The silence that greets me makes my blood run cold and I hold the torch up and search for any sign of my wife.

"Abi, answer me." I yell, but there is nothing back.

Suddenly, I hear a shout back from where we came, and I swear my heart almost gives out on me when I sense something has happened.

"We've got her."

"Drag the bastard back with us." I say through gritted teeth as I grab my fallen soldier and heave him over my shoulder, and we head back the way we came, the torch on our phones our only light.

It's as if we've been walking for hours before we hear voices ahead and I call out, the relief immense when I see my soldiers running toward us.

"Take him." I growl as I drop my soldier into their arms, praying we're not too late to save his life.

The relief is enormous when even more of my soldiers race toward me, all holding lit candles, lighting the tunnel and marking our way back.

"Where is she?" I growl and one of them says quickly, "In that fucking dungeon. She's with Cesare and…" he falters, and I growl. "And?"

"Um, Stephanie, boss."

At first I don't register the name and then the realization hits me hard. Cesare's Stephanie. The woman who disappeared off the face of the earth six months ago.

"She's here. What the fuck?"

The soldiers guide us back along the dark, dank tunnel and a shaft of light spills from the opening we jumped through. Strong arms reach down and pull us up one by one, and I waste no time in searching the room for the only person I want to see right now.

"Matteo." A desperate voice calls my name, and it's the sweetest sound as a hooded figure comes hurtling toward me and falls sobbing into my arms. The emotion that overwhelms me shocks me a little as my arms close around her shivering body so tightly, it's doubtful I will ever let her go.

I nuzzle my face into her hair and fight back the emotion as the relief hits me hard. She's safe. She's back with me where she belongs and, more importantly, she's alive.

The sound of raised voices catches my attention and I watch my soldiers dragging a kicking Mario out of his own pit and I shout, "Cuff that bastard to his own fucking altar!"

I watch, my hatred boiling like a simmering volcano as he is manhandled roughly onto the cruel hard stone and as Abigail's sobs subside, she pulls back and stares across the room at the man who almost took her from me.

I catch sight of Cesare holding another hooded figure close against his chest and as our eyes meet, I see the same murderous intent in my eyes reflected back at me. An unspoken sentence passes between us, and I lean down and say gently, "Trust me, princess. This won't take long."

She nods and whispers, "Make it hurt, Matteo. Make him pay for what he's done to every defenseless woman he's tortured and killed."

I nod with a surge of pride for my beautiful warrior wife because, far from crumbling, she is getting stronger by the second.

I glare at my nearest soldier and growl, "Don't take your eyes off her."

He nods, stepping to her side and draws his weapon as her protection. Not that I expect anything to happen to her in this room because it's filled with soldiers past and present who all appear to have one common purpose in mind. Mario.

Cesare steps by my side as we head toward the stone altar, and I stare into the crazed eyes of the man I hate most in the world.

The whip is still wrapped around his neck but has slackened enough for him to breathe and he hisses, "You're a fucking joke, Matteo. Do you really think you'll get away with this?"

"Get away with what?" I shrug, apparently unconcerned, and his eyes narrow. "You don't realize who you are dealing with. Back off and let the real men take control."

I nod to Cesare, who pulls him up by the whip and unwinds it from around his neck.

Mario laughs, his eyes flashing as he senses he's about to gain the upper hand. He probably thinks he already has it when he notices my father's soldiers that he has commanded up until this point.

"Tell me, Mario..." I say conversationally as Cesare begins to unfasten the metal cuffs that are currently holding him down.

"What was the plan regarding my wife?"

He grins and flicks his devious gaze over to Abi and sneers, "Power, Matteo. She will give me respectability because you can't kill me. If you do you will sign your own death warrant and your men know that." He turns and addresses the silent soldiers, watching the scene unfold with interest.

"Remember I am Giovanni's heir. It will be announced at the will reading in a matter of days. He told you so himself, and I am Don Ortega."

"How is that respectable, Mario?" I act confused. "Washington's finest won't allow a mafia boss in the heart of their inner circle. How is that your plan for supremacy?"

Mario laughs out loud as if I've said the funniest thing ever and then sneers, "Because they are as corrupt as I am. The Dark Lords is an organization that stretches to the highest office in the land. We look after our own, and that's why Jared Kensington gifted his daughter to me when she was sixteen. Jefferson stepped in and stole her from me, but you did me the biggest favor when you set him up. There was no other option but to honor the agreement our fathers made all those years ago and she became mine by default."

"But she didn't, Mario, because she married me." I shake my head and he grins.

"That is being annulled by Judge Stevenson as we speak."

Mario laughs out loud. "You see, a low life mafia wannabee has no power over the Dark Lords. If you kill me now, you won't be far behind me into hell."

I nod to Cesare who wraps the whip around Mario's neck and ties it into a noose and before Mario can react, he nods to two nearby soldiers who pull him roughly up as Cesare flings the end of the whip around a beam, tightening it so Mario swings high in the air.

He struggles as he grips the whip, loosening it enough to give him some air, and he roars, "You don't know who you are dealing with."

I growl, "I'm dealing with a dead man. A suicidal, sexually depraved man whose perverted games failed miserably. Just imagine the humiliation that will bring to your family, Mario. Plastered across the internet as the sexual deviant you are. Death by hanging in his own sex dungeon when his shameful game went wrong."

Mario struggles, his legs kicking in mid-air as Cesare pulls harder on the end of the whip and as we watch the thrashing naked body, fighting for his miserable life, I believe that every person in the room is enjoying watching the life drain from his wicked body.

It doesn't take long before his gurgled last gasp echoes around the room and as his body goes slack, a tidal wave of relief hits me as every single person here rejoices in his death.

Then it strikes me that one person is missing from this party and as I look around me, I growl, "Where the fuck is my stepmother?"

CHAPTER 30

ABIGAIL

For a moment there is silence before the room erupts into chaos as the soldiers spill in every direction, searching for the woman who is now Matteo's most wanted.

I stiffen as it all comes back to bite me, wondering if Matteo is desperate to have her back by his side where she belongs.

I move across to stand beside a shivering Stephanie and reach for her hand, both of us clutching the dark robes against our naked bodies as we shiver with a mixture of fear and the cold.

"Thank you." I whisper as we watch the scene unfold before us, both of us staring at the now limp body of a dictator.

"I'm glad he's dead." She hisses and I nod.

"Same."

We say no more because Matteo and Cesare appear before us and simultaneously tug us into their arms, the chaos surrounding us as they protect us in the eyes of the storm.

"I love you, princess."

I'm not sure I heard him correctly and must stiffen because

he pulls back and stares deep into my eyes, the love shining from his causing my breath to hitch.

"I love you." He whispers against my mouth and the tears release from their frozen prison and stream down my face.

He wipes them away with his finger and says gruffly, "I thought I'd lost you."

"Same." I gulp and, as his lips swallow my words, I kiss him with a mixture of relief and desperation.

He holds me close and kisses me so sweetly any chill inside me is turned to molten heat from his touch alone.

It's almost as if we are alone in a breaking storm and I want this moment to last forever.

As we break apart, I whisper, "I love you too."

For a second, we stare into one another's eyes and make a promise no man will ever break.

Then I remember my friend Clarice and gasp, "Clarice!"

"Who?"

Matteo is confused, and I whisper ungently. "My best friend. She was here, and they were torturing her. Do you think she's…?"

I can't even say the word and Matteo calls out, "Search this fucking place from top to bottom. If you find anyone, bring them here."

The remaining soldiers jump to attention and head off, sweeping this place for bodies, dead or alive.

I catch sight of Cesare holding Stephanie closer and Matteo follows my gaze and smiles when he sees the emotion on his friend's face.

"You said Diana was here." I interrupt the tender moment and wish I hadn't when his face clouds with rage.

"She brought us here, and I'm guessing it was for this reason. She wanted Mario gone, and we were her best shot at making it happen."

Stephanie looks across and says loudly, "Diana told me what to do when Abigail arrived."

We turn to stare at her in shock as Cesare says softly, "Tell us, baby."

She nods, smiling up at him with a look of happiness that brings tears to my eyes and as we step closer, she says in her soft voice, "When Mario brought me here, it wasn't only to clean for him. I was one of many girls he abducted off the street to use in his sick fantasies."

From the expression on Cesare's face, it's a good job Mario's dead already and Stephanie sighs heavily. "Diana was no better. They used us and made us do things I can't even form the words to describe. Parties mainly with men like Mario and Diana was the perfect hostess. He soon started getting wilder, darker, and the games began to change. He dreamed up this Dark Lords shit, and we had to perform in his ceremonies. If we tried to escape, that girl was the next one chained to the stone altar and her life was dragged out in the coldest and most callous way."

She shivers and whispers, "It was easier to go along with him. It would be over, and he would leave, sometimes for weeks at a time. During his absence, we were all locked on the top floor of the house where there were no windows and only enough food to last until he returned."

Matteo mutters, "I wish we had made it more painful for the sick fucking bastard."

Cesare nods, looking sick and emotional as he reaches for Stephanie's hand.

"It surprised me when Diana pulled me aside the last time they were here and told me if he ever brought a woman here and said she was going to be his wife, I was to save her."

I shake my head. "I don't understand. Why would she do that?"

"Because Diana loved him." Matteo interrupts. "She wanted

him all to herself and was jealous. She knew that if he married you, she would no longer be in a position of power. He would have no further need of her, especially if he was right and became Don Ortega at the reading of my father's will. It was her insurance policy, and it paid off."

"So, Diana saved me." I can't process what I'm hearing and Matteo growls, "No. She saved herself and getting Stephanie to be your guardian angel, ensured the utmost chaos when you both entered the room. It's obvious she used you as a distraction to escape and is, no doubt, speeding as far away from here as possible, ready to make her next move."

It all slots into place and I note the resignation in Matteo's eyes as he comes to the realization that she has slipped away from him.

Stephanie nods. "Diana was equally as cruel as Mario, if not worse. She was a vindictive bitch who delighted in torturing the sacrifices herself. There was no compassion in that woman, which tells me you are right. She did this for her own reasons, and you should be afraid of them."

We are distracted when two soldiers appear, guiding a familiar face into the room, and I cry out as I run toward the only friend I ever had.

"Clarice!" She is wrapped in a similar black robe and her face is streaked with tears. Her breath coming in gasps as she winces with pain.

"Abi." She openly sobs as she whispers between them, "Please forgive me."

"Of course, I forgive you." I crush her to me, noting her squeal of pain and then she says in shock, "Is that…?"

I turn and see Mario's body swinging the short distance away, and I nod. "Yes."

She stiffens and I'm surprised when she gasps, "Oh my God. What have you done?"

Matteo is by my side in an instant and says roughly, "What do you mean?"

Clarice stares at us in fear and whispers, "You won't get away with this."

"We already have." Matteo snaps and she looks so afraid it's as if my heart is held in an icy glove as she sobs, "The supreme Dark Lord is his father. Nothing can save you."

"What do you mean? Sam Bachini is no supreme dark lord."

Matteo scoffs and Clarice shakes her head, looking as if she wants to run from the scene.

"Sam Bachini isn't his father."

"Then who is?" Matteo says roughly, and Clarice shrugs.

"I don't know his name, but Jefferson told me Mario has more power than any of them. He was set to inherit the title of Supreme Dark Lord when his father dies, and they are all powerless to refuse him anything."

"Where's Jefferson now?" I ask quickly, knowing he was with Clarice in New York, and she sobs, "I don't know."

I stare at Matteo in confusion and from the look on his face this is unwelcome news to him and then more soldiers crowd into the chamber and report back.

"We have ten women all wearing black robes and are scared as fuck. They all tell the same story. They were taken off the streets and brought here to serve Mario and Diana."

"Any other names?" Matteo asks, and the soldier shakes his head. "None."

"Take them home and make a note of their addresses. We may need to call on them for more information. Make sure you get their story before they leave. We have a man hunt to conduct."

I turn to Matteo and note the worry in his eyes and my heart sinks when I realize we have only made an impossible situation worse. We don't even know who we're dealing with, and it appears the answers lie back where I came from.

I reach for his hand and say with determination.

"I think it's time to go home."

He stares at me long and hard and then nods, knowing exactly what I'm getting at, and he shouts to a nearby soldier, "Take this woman to the apartment and make her comfortable. Don't let her out of your sight and get her medical attention from our usual doctor."

The soldier springs forward and takes Clarice's arm and the panic in her eyes makes me say with a comforting smile, "It's ok. You'll be safe there. Probably safer than at home. Just tell us what you can remember, every small detail, whether you think it relevant or not. We'll figure a way out of this."

She nods and says falteringly, "I'm sorry, Abi."

"It's ok." I smile, but my heart has hardened toward the girl I once regarded as a close friend. No matter what her reasons were, she still betrayed me and it's doubtful I will ever truly forgive her for that.

As she walks away, Matteo slips his arm around my shoulders and says softly, "Let's go home."

CHAPTER 31

MATTEO

What a fucking day. I am still struggling to make sense of it all and as we leave Mario to burn in hell, I head home with my wife safely by my side. Cesare and Stephanie take the car in front and as Abigail snuggles beside me, it's good to shut the whole world out.

"I was so afraid I'd never see you again." She whimpers, the tears sliding down her face as she turns to face me.

I stroke away her tears and whisper, "I would search every corner of the universe until I found you. I meant what I said back at that house of horrors. I love you."

Her eyes widen and I dip my head and press my mouth against her heavenly lips and as the black robe parts, her shivering body presses against mine and she whispers, "I love you too and I am proud to be your wife."

With a low moan, I kiss her deeply and with a hunger that I must suppress for now. She has been through torture, and I will tread carefully until she heals.

Most of the journey is spent holding Abi. I can't let her go and just contemplating what may have happened back at that hellish house makes my blood run cold.

Abi is silent beside me, and I'm worried about her. I'm used to the shit this life throws up daily, but she isn't. All her life she has been protected and shielded from the dark side and now she has faced it head on, with a front-row seat that must have affected her.

She snuggles closer and whispers, "I'm still amazed my father is involved with this Dark Lord's situation. He just doesn't seem the type."

As I remember what Dom told me about his experience with the Dark Lords, I'm doubtful this was just Mario's twisted mind acting out his fantasies. However, I agree. It does seem surprising that Jared Kensington would don a black robe and carry out illegal acts for the sake of a club he belongs to and yet he sold his daughter. He must have some serious heat on him to make him do that.

"Do you think my mother knows?"

Abigail probes and I sigh heavily, rubbing her shoulder while I try to make sense of my thoughts.

"Possibly not. I heard he has a connection with Judge Stevenson and Sam Bachini."

"It may not be what Mario told us, and is something perfectly innocent."

Her voice lifts with hope, which makes me feel like a bastard because obviously it's not innocent at all.

"Do you think?"

I drop a light kiss on top of her head and try to inject some reassurance into my voice. "Listen, Mario controlled a damaged, evil mind and would have made a saint appear corrupt to suit his own ends. Only your father can tell you what this is really about and I'm guessing if he realized what you went through, he would be enraged."

"I suppose."

Abigail sighs. "I still can't believe Clarice was involved. She always told me she hated Jefferson. Why did she want to be his wife?"

"Power perhaps. It's a lethal drug that many overdose on. My own father was obsessed. Diana too. It makes people do the most unbelievable things when it's within their grasp. I'm guessing that's the reason for this whole shit show and whoever Mario's father turns out to be is the one wielding most of it."

"Do you have any idea who he is?"

"No. It may even be Sam Bachini for all I know, and Mario fabricated that as well. I'm guessing Jefferson could help us with that, so it's important we find the bastard and discover what he knows."

I remember the man who crawled across the room back at my club with disgust. He will always crawl through life, taking what he can without earning a cent of it. He's the worst kind of man and hides his corrupt soul behind designer suits and fancy living. At least people understand what they get with me. I don't pretend to be anything else, which makes him the most dangerous kind of criminal.

I'm not surprised when Abigail falls asleep and I'm glad of it. She has been through so much and is probably exhausted.

As her head falls to my lap, I pull out my phone and text my brothers.

> Matteo
>
> This Dark Lord's shit is driving me insane. Mario is no longer a problem but threw something up I need checking out. His parentage.

> **DOM**
>
> I feel you, brother. I'm still scraping that shit off my soul. I'll ask Flora what she knows. Good job with Mario. I hope he's enjoying his new home.

We must be careful what we say over text, and this thread will be deleted almost immediately.

Leo's reply follows immediately.

> **LEO**
>
> I'll do some digging. Regarding my own plans, the target is taking a short vacation before our meeting in a few days' time. It may be the appropriate time to pay him a visit.

Knowing we will feel a lot better when we know what is written in our father's will, that can't come soon enough for me and then Leo texts.

> **LEO**
>
> Any news on Diana?

> **MATTEO**
>
> Missing presumed plotting our downfall.

I type back, my mind switching to Diana and the reasons behind her involvement in this. Something isn't adding up and I still don't believe she wanted Mario dead. It doesn't make sense because she loved him so much, she would do anything he asked.

There is something we aren't seeing, and it may be standing hidden in full view. I'm guessing the answer lies with Mario's parentage and that is the most important thing right now. To discover who Mario Bachini really is and then I'm guessing it will all slot into place and the blurred picture will become a lot clearer.

> **LEO**
> Keep us informed but move fast. We're missing a vital piece of the puzzle that could be the difference between success and failure.
> There's too much at stake for failure to be an option.

> **DOM**
> With you, brother.

> **MATTEO**
> Me too.

As I delete the thread, I stare out of the window and wish this shit was over already. More than anything, I want to lock Abi in a room and keep her safe. If anything happens to her because of my family I will never forgive myself and yet something is telling me this isn't over by a long way and it will be up to me and my two brothers to figure it all out.

CHAPTER 32

ABIGAIL

I'm exhausted and physically ache everywhere. When the car arrives at the underground car park, I am so happy to be home. It's funny how I think of this as my home now. The thought of returning to Washington and my family fills me with fear because something lurks in the shadows there that isn't in my best interests.

As soon as we step into the elevator, I lean against Matteo and say with concern. "Where is Stephanie?"

"With Cesare. He'll make sure she's ok before we deal with business."

"I'm so happy they are together again."

Matteo pulls me tighter against him and whispers huskily, "If he has even half the feelings I have for you, he must be ecstatic."

I smile up at him and as the elevator stops and opens into his apartment, I shiver. "I need a long hot bath and to burn this fucking robe."

Matteo's eyes flash as I step out of it and leave it on the floor of the elevator and walk naked into his apartment. His low hiss makes me turn and his eyes flash with anger when he notes the bruises decorating my body, courtesy of Mario's boot.

"That fucking bastard." His voice is so low it slides over my soul like one of Satan's demons and in this moment, I see the man I love in all his glory. Dark, dangerous and deadly, but with something Mario would never have, honor.

"Come with me."

I hold out my hand, noting the gleam in his eyes as he reaches for my hand and as we head to his bedroom, I have only one thing on my mind.

We step into the huge bathroom, and I set about filling the tub and say suggestively, "Why are you still dressed?"

His delight is evident but is quickly replaced with concern and he says, "It's too soon. You've been through a lot…"

I hold up my hand. "I need you, Matteo. Life is too short to wait for things you want the most if they are within your grasp. If anything, I've learned that lesson and what scared me the most through the whole ordeal was that I would never get this opportunity again."

I step forward and take his hand, saying softly, "To love you."

As the steam fills the bathroom, the heat from his gaze surrounds me in a warm glow, and I watch as he shrugs off his jacket and tosses his shirt to the ground. I salivate at the sight of that toned body, rippling with power as he holds my gaze with his lustful one and reaches for his belt. I shiver when he drops his pants and stands in naked splendor before me and tugs me close in one sudden sharp move and says firmly, "Then we take it slow. Just sweet, gentle loving, until you heal."

He dips his mouth to my neck and sucks my needy flesh, and I swear my heart flutters. I never expected to be so turned on by a man like him. A man who wears danger like a badge and is unapologetic in life. I love the scuff from his jaw grazing against my delicate skin and his hard muscles flexing under my touch, the deep groans and hard rigid cock demonstrating how much I affect him.

I never thought in a million years that a man like Matteo Ortega would be my future and I am desperate to take advantage of every second I'm with him for the rest of my life.

I am so consumed with desire and an aching need to worship him and drop to my knees and guide his throbbing cock into my mouth.

"Abi, you don't have to…" I squeeze his balls tightly and he groans. "Fuck me."

It makes me smile as I lick and suck, coaxing his pleasure out to deal with my demons for me.

He holds my head and thrusts in hard, violently even, and I love every second of it. To anyone watching it would appear degrading, but to me it's everything I want in life. Worshipping this man. My master.

He is rock-hard and can't be far off and as he makes to pull out, I grip his ass hard and pull him in deeper, his cock hitting the back of my throat causing him to roar, "Oh fuck!" as he shoots so hard down my throat I'm momentarily stunned. It keeps coming in glorious waves and fills me from the inside out before trickling down the side of my jaw as I desperately suck him dry.

By the time he finishes, I am so turned on and keen to carry on all night. I'm insatiable. I want him every way I can and as I fall back and stare up at him, the gleam in his obsidian eyes makes me smile.

"You're a wicked woman, Mrs. Ortega." His twisted grin makes me laugh and I lie back on the floor naked and unashamed.

"I'm *your* wicked woman, Mr. Ortega, and I want to know what you're going to do about that."

"Well, first…" he nods to the tub that is about to spill its contents over the floor. "I'm going to save us from an expensive clean-up operation."

He shuts off the water and stands, gazing down at my wanton body spread out on the floor, begging him to deal with it.

"Then I'm going to bring my wife in line."

I shiver in anticipation as he reaches down and pulls me up, so I'm flush against his body and he runs his hands down to my ass and pushes his finger in slowly. I bite my lip as he enters a space I never thought was a thing and the forbidden nature of it makes me immediately wet.

He brushes his thumb against my clit and whispers darkly, "I'm going to punish you for taking something without permission."

I gasp as he lifts me into his arms and kisses me long and hard and then cry out as he dumps me unceremoniously into the tub, the water splashing onto the tiled floor at his feet.

He drops down by the side of the tub and holds me firmly down, before taking the bar of soap and rubbing it against my body with a husky, "You need cleaning up, princess, and when you shine, I'm going to worship this body like it deserves."

I shiver with expectation as he gently massages the sweet-smelling soap into my skin, then he captures my lips in his and kisses me so softly, sweetly and seductively, I swear my entire body shivers.

He pulls back and stares deep into my eyes and whispers, "I don't deserve a woman like you."

I reach up and stroke his face, loving every inch of skin that makes this man perfect in my eyes and whisper, "You deserve the best, Mr. Ortega, and so do I. It's why this works."

His eyes flash as he reaches down and lifts me clean out of the tub and carries me dripping in every sense of the word into the large bedroom. As he lowers me gently onto the bed, his eyes flare with passion as he whispers, "I'm going to take my time loving you."

He stares at me with so much tenderness my breath catches as he strokes my skin with a reverence that makes my heart flutter. As he kisses me softly from my head right down to my toes, I lie back and enjoy every amazing second of his love.

This *is* love. I'm in no doubt about that, as he worships every inch of my skin, taking extra care when he reaches my bruises. Then he worships me inside, as his tongue flicks against my clit and gently sucks it, manipulating it to his bidding as I fall apart under him. I can't hold back the orgasm that shakes my entire soul as I greedily accept the pleasure he gives me.

It will never be enough, though. He's like a drug that merely increases desire, not sate it and as he lifts my leg and places it on his shoulder, it feels so wicked seeing a warrior like him deep between my legs.

When his rigid cock pushes against my drenched pussy, I almost cry with relief. This is what I want, him inside me because in that moment he is all mine. Completely and irrevocably all mine, nobody between us, even business. In these moments, we shut the whole world out and nothing can touch us because we are one person, and it feels fucking amazing.

CHAPTER 33

MATTEO

I fuck my wife for two solid hours. There is no part of her that doesn't feel my mark. I fuck her, then worship her, in between kissing her and then worshipping her again until her body responds on repeat. It's as if I can't get enough and I swear I've never cum so hard in my life, or as many times. She brings out the best of me along with the beast in me and I still can't believe I got so lucky. I should be tending to business. It's always business first in my life. But nothing tops the moments I'm deep inside my wife and time can stand still and wait for me because nothing is more important than her.

It makes me smile when she begs me to stop, so exhausted she can barely keep her eyes open, her pussy swollen from overuse and her skin flushed and raw from my rough jaw and hands. I have used and abused my wife to the point of exhaustion and so I tuck the sheets around her and whisper, "Sleep, princess. You're safe here."

She barely even smiles before she falls into a deep sleep, telling me I have a few hours at least to wrap this shit up.

I shower and change, loving how every inch of me inside

and out is firing on all cylinders. It's as if she has supercharged my batteries because I could take on the world right now.

I dress for business in my customary black suit and, anchoring my gun to my side, I adjust my mood to bastard.

* * *

As I head into the living room, I tap out a text, and it doesn't take long for my closest friend to appear by my side. Like me, he appears able to take on a war single-handedly, and I grin when I see the effect his woman has on him. Yes, life is good, but it could be better and as we head from the apartment, we both know what we must do.

The journey to my penthouse on the other side of town is spent going over the plan. When it's to my satisfaction, I say with interest. "How's Stephanie?"

Cesare's eyes flash as he hisses, "As well as can be expected, despite what that bastard put her through."

"Has she said any more about that?"

Cesare shakes his head. "It wasn't the right time to start asking questions."

I nod because he deserves his time with her. They both do and, dragging up what happened can wait until she's stronger.

We stop outside my penthouse and take the elevator to the private floor, wondering what Abi's friend is going to think when we burst inside. She has also been through hell, but I can't forgive a traitor and she is the worst kind. A best friend who sold out her sister for personal gain. She is the worst kind of human in my eyes and being female isn't going to help her now. Abi may have forgiven her to a degree, but I never will because she put my wife's life in danger and took her to a place she may never shake from her mind.

My soldier on duty jumps to attention when we head into the room and I say gruffly, "Where is she?"

"Sleeping, boss."

I nod and stride to the bedroom, slamming open the door, causing her to jump up with a panicked, "Fuck! What's happening?"

I kick the door shut and Cesare moves to the bed and pulls her out roughly, forcing her to sit in a chair by the window.

Her eyes are wide and fearful as I sit on the bed and stare at her hard.

"Jefferson."

"What about him?"

Her lip trembles as I hiss, "Call him and tell him you'll meet him back at your father's apartment. Tell him Mario's dead and you're frightened."

She nods, biting her lip with nerves and I growl, "Get dressed."

Cesare releases her and she almost runs to the closet and returns minutes later dressed in one of the outfits that I keep for visitors. This place has often entertained prisoners, people I need to remove from life until I can deal with them. The odd whore who I fuck to keep me calm and the occasional woman who charms her way into my bed for one night only. Women like Demelza who use their cunning to trap a beast but end up used and abused and sent on their way desperate for more. Daughters of men who owe me favors, who I seduce and send back to daddy broken and yearning to repeat the experience. This place is pure business, and I will never bring Abi here. She is pure pleasure and will be the only woman I fuck for the rest of my life.

I can tell Clarice is scared shitless, which is exactly what I need her to be and so we stand either side of her and retrace our steps, this time heading for her apartment not far from here.

The journey to her apartment is interesting when she says fearfully, "I can't believe he's dead."

"Best place for him," I growl, and she stutters, "Aren't you scared?"

Cesare laughs out loud at the foolish statement given who she sits between, and I say with amusement, "Why? Should I be?"

"But his father. He's the Supreme Dark Lord. He's wicked."

"That makes two of us then."

I move suddenly and grip her face so hard it makes her eyes water and growl, "What was Jefferson's plan the night of the gala?"

She shakes and as I release her, she whispers, "I was to make contact with Abi and lure her away from you. Jefferson and Mario would be waiting and steal her from under your nose."

My eyes darken and she begins to shake.

"Jefferson told me it was for her own good. She was to marry Mario under the orders of the Dark Lord, and you had stepped in the way of that. He was angry and if I helped put her where she belongs, I would be rewarded."

She gulps. "Jefferson promised to marry me instead, and I would enjoy what came with it. He was so persuasive and made it the most desirable thing in the world and I believed him. He told me he had always wanted me but was going along with the plan until Mario was in place. He never wanted Abigail, he wanted me, and I was the fool who believed every lying word."

I don't even feel sorry for her and shake my head at how foolish she was. "So, you sold your own friend for personal gain. You wanted what she had and didn't even consider it was wrong."

"I thought it was right."

She shakes her head sadly. "They told me you had stepped in the middle and needed to be removed. Her father had agreed to the arrangement and was pissed you ruined their carefully laid plans. What was I to think? I have lived in that world my entire life and understand how it works. Relationships are made for business, nothing else and I thought Abigail knew that too. We are expected to know our place, which is heading up the household of a powerful man. Being the trophy wife who never questions her husband and plays the model wife in public, while allowing her husband to do what the fuck he wants. To turn a blind eye and deal with it behind closed doors. This is our fucking life, and I thought Abigail accepted it."

Cesare stares at her with scorn and, if anything, I hate her even more. She has none of the fire and brave heart of my wife which certainly makes this easier.

We reach her father's apartment and head inside, the doorman turning his head in the other direction when he notes the company she's keeping.

We step inside another penthouse, and I growl, "Call him."

She wastes no time and picks up the phone and dials a number and her voice shakes as she whispers, "Jefferson."

I point to the phone, and she places it on speaker, and I hear the pathetic whining of the man I want to kill with my bare hands.

"Fuck, Clarice, what's happening? Mario's not answering his phone and you've gone missing. Nobody is answering at the house and I'm going out of my mind."

"I have news." She says in a soft whisper.

"I can't talk on the phone, though. You must meet me at my father's apartment."

"Fuck, Clarice. I don't like this. Can't you just tell me now?"

"No!" she yells, the panic real in her voice. "Please, Jefferson." She sobs into the phone. "I need you."

There's a tense silence before he says with a heavy sigh.

"I'll be there in ten."

He cuts the call and I nod to Cesare, who wastes no time in gripping Clarice hard and pulling her hands behind her back.

"What the–" she screams as he slaps tape over her mouth

and binds her wrists behind her back, before doing the same to her feet.

She stares at me with fear as I nod, and he forces her into a chair and ties her to it so she can't move or speak.

As soon as she's secured, we take up our positions behind the door and wait silently for the bastard to arrive.

True to his word, the elevator opens inside of ten minutes and as soon as he steps into the apartment, Clarice is the first thing he sees.

His shocked "Fuck!" barely leaves his lips before he turns to run, and we step in his way, and I growl. "Hello, Jefferson."

Cesare wastes no time and punches him square in the jaw and as he stumbles, roughly cuffs his hands and forces him down onto the couch, facing Clarice, before pressing his gun to his head.

The fact Jefferson pisses himself doesn't go unnoticed, and I stare at him with disgust as I sit astride a chair in the center of the room.

"I want information."

Jefferson stutters, "I don't–" Cesare strikes him hard against the head and busts his nose, the blood spurting down his face, his agonized scream telling me it hurts like hell.

"Who is Mario's father?"

Jefferson starts to shake, and the sound of Clarice sobbing is the sweetest sound.

"I don't know his name."

"Then tell me about Sam Bachini. What's the relationship with your father?"

Jefferson stutters, "They were friends at college. There were three of them. My father, Jared and Sam."

"Tell me about their connection and don't hold anything back."

Jefferson nods, accepting it's the best way out of an impossible situation.

"They help each other out. My father is close to Jared, but they tried to distance themselves from Sam."

"Why?"

"Because he's a criminal. My father's a Judge and Jared is a respectable businessman. Sam Bachini brings more heat than the desert and they didn't want to be associated with him."

That would explain why Abigail only met them once, which confuses me a little.

"I thought their moms were friends."

"I don't know about that. I was warned not to get too close to Mario. He is bad news, and it wouldn't help my career if I was considered his friend. I was to marry Abigail and our families would pull together and make sure I was given a position of power."

"What can you tell me about the Dark Lords?" I drop the name into the conversation like a cluster bomb.

Jefferson acts as if I just killed his pet and says in a whisper, "Our fathers belong to it. It's an organization made up of powerful men, a club of sorts, that helps one another out. I swear that's all I know."

"So, you weren't involved in their sick rituals."

"I don't understand."

I glance across at Clarice, who knows only too well what they involve, and I growl, "What about, Clarice? You promised her Abi's ring on her finger if she got her away from me. What was that all about?"

Jefferson peers across at Clarice and shrugs. "She was convenient. Mario came to me and told me that unless I cooperated, his father would make sure my father was ruined and any future I had would be on the streets. He told me to use Clarice to get to Abigail and promise her the world in return for her cooperation."

He sneers. "She was always a willing fuck, anyway, and would do anything to be my girl, so it was easy."

He yells when Cesare punches him again and it makes me smile because Cesare hates disrespecting women more than anyone I've ever met, and Jefferson's words are like a red rag to a bull.

Clarice sobs louder and I shake my head as I regard the foolish woman who believed everything they told her and I turn back to Jefferson and say calmly, "Well, Mario's dead, so what now?"

I'm interested to watch his reaction and note the blood draining from an already pale face as he says in disbelief, "How?"

I shrug. "He was a victim of his own sick games. He won't be missed."

Jefferson stares at me in shock and whispers, "I don't understand."

It's obvious to me he doesn't, and he says slowly, "My father always spoke of another man. A friend of Sam who he appeared to fear."

"Did he give you a name?" Now I'm interested and Jefferson shakes his head.

"No. I overheard him talking to Jared one day when they thought nobody was listening. They said that Sam was out of control and Mario's father wouldn't be happy about that but I don't know his identity."

"Can you find out?" I say sharply and Jefferson looks worried.

I lean a little closer and say darkly, "Let me rephrase that question. The only way you get out of this is to work for me. You head home, do some digging and find me a name. When it checks out, you're off the hook and nothing more will be said. The recording I have of you will be returned and you won't see me again."

I turn to Clarice and snarl. "Same for you. Work together if you must but find what I need. Mario is dead and you will be next if I don't have that information in hours. Tell anyone about this and you'll be saying hi to Mario in the afterlife and like his passing, yours won't be pleasant."

I nod to Cesare, who unties Jefferson before doing the same to Clarice, and we stare at their shivering bodies as I say darkly, "Don't make me come and find you again. There will be no second chances next time. All I want is a name and you can sleep easy at night."

Cesare places my business card on the table, and we leave without a backward glance.

Something is telling me that name will be mine in a matter of hours.

CHAPTER 34

ABIGAIL

When Matteo returns, I am relaxing in the tub, trying to ease the burn. It's as if my entire body is on fire and it hurts inside and out. The beating I was gifted by Mario is starting to reveal itself, and the way Matteo tore through my body leaves a different kind of pain.

He enters the room and drops down on his heels beside the bath, staring at me with lust in his eyes.

"Hey, beautiful. Did you miss me?"

"Of course." I gaze up at him shyly, which is a joke when I think back on what we've done and he lightly touches his lips to mine and whispers, "We need to eat."

I nod, grateful for food because I can't remember the last meal I ate and as he helps me from the tub, he wraps a warm towel around me and pulls me close, kissing me softly which banishes any thought of food from my mind in an instance.

"Tell me why I want you, Matteo?"

I gaze at him shyly and he appears confused at my question. I reach up and lay my hand flat on his face and do the same with the other one. As I hold his gorgeous face in my hands, I marvel at it. So strong, violent even, and I stare into those obsidian eyes and drown in danger. He is volatile, rough and yet so sexy my heart flutters every time he is by my side and there is never any moment of the day that I don't want him to fuck me senseless.

"You are so wrong for me and yet I can't imagine ever walking away. You are like the eye of the storm and the thunder in the sky. Deadly but breath-taking at the same time and an impossible madness. Why is it the most important thing in my life to make this work, even if it means walking away from everything I know?"

His hand snaps against mine and my breath hitches at the desire stirring the demon inside him. His eyes glitter as he whispers, "Because I'm your perfect madness. You are my queen and when two people meet who were meant for one another, they are a force of nature to be reckoned with. You bring out the best and worst of me and nothing can take you away from me all the time you want to be by my side. If you change your mind, it will ruin me, which is why it's important never to give you a reason to walk away."

His voice scratches against my heart, tapping until it finds a way in.

"I can't imagine ever not wanting you. I can't ever picture walking away from you and I'm only wondering if my body can stand the number of times I want you inside it."

His low laugh makes me smile and I love it when he grips my head tightly and bites down softly on my lower lip, causing me to groan as he whispers huskily, "When you have healed, I want to demonstrate the pleasure I can bring to your body. The power of domination, not in a sadistic way."

I shiver at the memory of another man's idea of domination and Matteo strokes my face and whispers, "I will never hurt you, princess. You are the most precious thing in my world and it's my job to cherish that. To make you happy and bloom under my touch. To protect and fight for you when nobody else will. To make you happy and safe and paste a permanent smile on your lips. I may not have experienced much of that growing up, but I realize its power. You have polished my soul and made me want to be a better man just to prove that I am worthy of keeping you."

Pressing my lips to his, I kiss him lovingly and it's different somehow. As if we are reciting our marriage vows and this time they come from the heart. The moment when I devote my life to my husband, because if I know only one thing, it's that I have fallen hard and deep for the warrior in my arms.

Carefully, I push his jacket from his body and the cold steel of the gun rests against my naked body. It grazes my breasts and I shiver with desire. Dropping to my knees, I unzip his pants and take out his cock and caress it with a reverence that makes him hiss as his cum leaks at the tip.

I slide it home, loving the way he fills me entirely and as I worship my man on my knees, there is no shame involved. Just pure love because I want to give him double the pleasure he gives me and as he thrusts hard against the back of my throat, I adore every second of it. He fists my hair and pumps in hard, fast, and furious, as if he's using me for pleasure. I *want* him to use me, to get off on what I can do, and I moan against his velvet shaft as he gifts me his attention, and experience a tidal wave of emotion that pours down my throat.

"Fuck." He groans as he empties inside my mouth and as I swallow, I relish the sensation as it glides like a river through my body.

If I spend the rest of my life on my knees before this warrior, I will die happy, and I never really expected to fall unconditionally in love with a man like him.

Matteo pulls me up and kisses me so deeply it makes my toes curl, and he returns the favor by dropping to his knees and spreading my legs. Then he reminds me just how good he is with that wicked tongue as he coaxes the most delicious soul shattering orgasm from inside my burning body, causing me to moan like a tortured soul denied entrance to heaven and then I come so hard it nearly brings me to my knees.

As my body shakes, he wastes no time in swinging me into his arms and lowering me back into the warm water, where I watch him strip before joining me.

He settles behind me and wraps those strong arms around my satiated body and pouring some soap on his hands, proceeds to wash my entire body with slow sensuous movements that bring me even deeper under his spell.

"Never leave me, princess."

His low growl rests against my ear like a promise dressed in threats and I smile, loving how possessive my man is and not really believing I deserve it.

"How could I leave love, Matteo?"

He carries on massaging the soap into my body and I whisper, "When I was growing up, I read stories about when the princess finds her prince. It all seemed so normal, as if that was a certainty in life. Then, when my parents told me I was to marry Jefferson, I was confused. I didn't love him and I sure as hell knew he didn't love me. I asked my mom about it, and she told me angrily that love was just an excuse to make bad decisions. It messed up futures and had no place in our world."

Matteo whispers, "She sounds like my father."

I stroke his leg as it presses against me and whisper, "Then I feel sorry for them both. Because I wouldn't trade these feelings for all the money and power in the world. If anything, this is the real power. The kind that makes a person invincible to protect the greatest emotion in the world."

I turn and stare into his glittering eyes and whisper, "I love you, Matteo Ortega, and I would do absolutely anything for you. I just want you to know that."

He appears almost emotional as he whispers, "I never believed love was going to feature in my life until I met you.

Now I understand why we all chase the impossible dream, hoping to find it one day. I never did, and that's why I've fallen so hard for you, princess, because you have given me something money can never buy. You accept me for who I am and love me regardless and for a man who has nobody ever look at him the way you look at me, tells me I am never letting you go. You're stuck with me, and I pity the poor bastard who ever tries to interfere with that because you are mine, and I will do anything for you except allow you to walk away."

His eyes flash with a possession that should scare the hell out of me, but I understand it. It's a possessive fury that I share. What we have found is so amazing it hurts me to even think about losing it and I wrap my hand around it and hold on tight because I feel exactly the same.

Words are no longer necessary. We both know what this is and so I turn and rest my head against his chest, while my man takes care of me in the sweetest way. The water laps against our naked bodies and the silence washes across our battered souls and as I fall even deeper in love with my husband, I know I will never be alone again.

CHAPTER 35

MATTEO

Abigail is worried. I know because she hasn't spoken a word since we boarded my jet, and she took a seat by the window. I sit beside her with Cesare opposite. Stephanie has remained at home to heal, and I know he hates every minute he is away from her side. I understand his emotion because I feel it too. If Abi isn't connected to me, it's as if my air supply has been pulled and I struggle to breathe.

We discuss business for most of the flight and Abi listens to every word; the worry deepening in her eyes as we go over the facts.

I realize she is nervous about facing her parents and I don't blame her. They have been hiding secrets that concern her and as the jet begins its descent, she grips my hand tightly and whispers, "What if this doesn't work?"

"It will."

I sound so confident I even fool myself. There are so many unidentified factors that could come into play, and I know Cesare is also concerned.

As the jet touches down in Washington, I am nervous, which surprises me. I don't do nerves. I never have and yet something is scaring the shit out of me and I'm guessing it's because I'm taking Abi back to a life that may reach out and tear her from mine.

My cars are waiting and as we spill from the plane and take our usual seats, I prepare myself for a confrontation that could end badly for all of us.

Once again, I check my phone for any texts from Jefferson, but nothing comes through and the ball of anger inside me is growing by the second because what is taking him so long to deliver the information that will save his life?

It doesn't take long before we reach the palatial home of the woman who is nervously wrapped in her own thoughts as we turn into the driveway.

The security gates open and we sweep through them as if we are welcome and I'm guessing our stay here won't be the usual one when a bride brings her husband home for the very first time.

Abi's hand finds mine and squeezes it reassuringly before she whispers, "I will stand by you, whatever happens. I just want you to know that."

Her words light a fire inside my soul because she is relying on me, and I won't let her down.

Raising her hand to my lips, I deliver my response with actions, not words, and as the car rolls to a stop, she says with a sigh. "Showtime."

The door opens, and I reach for her hand and help her from the car, loving how beautiful she is as she steps into the sunshine. Her sandy hair has been pulled back into a sophisticated ponytail and the sun reflects off the highlights in her hair. Her simple cream dress dusts her knees and the diamond on her finger sparkles as it catches the light. She stands high on designer heels and smiles bravely as she catches my eye and I watch the confidence grow even greater as she fixes her eyes on her childhood home. and appears a little confused.

"It feels different coming back.'

"In what way?" I answer as we head up the stone steps leading to the huge wooden door.

"It doesn't feel like home anymore." She appears puzzled by that and yet I love hearing it. Her home is with me now and I suppose that's the first hurdle jumped because I was worried she would look at me differently when she returned to her palace.

The door swings open and a uniformed maid almost bows as we enter a billionaire's paradise and I stare around at luxury on a very grand scale. A large hallway stretches endlessly into the distance with a sweeping staircase the main focus of the room, branching off either side as it leads to the other floors.

"Welcome home, Miss. Abigail."

The maid says respectfully and Abigail smiles sweetly but says with determination, "Actually, it's Mrs. Ortega now. Meet my husband, Matteo."

She pulls me by her side, and I'm surprised at the pleasant smile on the maid's face as she grins and says, "Congratulations. I am so happy for you."

It confuses me a little because she appears delighted, and a look passes between them that tells me there is one person in this house who is on Abi's side, at least.

As we follow her through the immense luxurious space, I'm struck by how different this life is to mine. I enjoy luxury, but it's at the cost of battered souls. This is purer somehow, more impressive and way out of my league.

"Don't be impressed by this, Matteo." Abi shocks me by whispering. "Obviously, this has all come at a bloody price and may appear respectable but cost more than money."

I nod because she has reminded me exactly what's at stake and if anything, at least I don't pretend to be something I'm not.

As we enter a huge light-filled reception room, it's as if the atmosphere changes and I'm hit with hostility the minute I walk in beside my wife.

"Abigail." Jared's deep tone greets us, but there is no warmth attached and I stare with interest at a man who is hiding many secrets of his own.

Abi grips my hand a little tighter and stares at her disapproving parents and says defiantly, "Daddy, mommy um, you remember my husband, Matteo, don't you?"

The fact she's just dropped a bomb into their perfect world makes me wonder why it doesn't explode in their faces because, if anything, they already know.

Jared sighs and points to the couch and says with a firm voice, "Take a seat. This won't take long."

We sit side by side, our hands entwined, and I observe the scene with interest because there is nothing he could say that will change what's happening.

"I heard you were married."

He sighs as he sits beside his wife, who appears to have frozen into stone. When we walked into the room, she looked as if a bad smell invaded her perfect world, which angered me more than any words she could speak. Women like Anna Kensington bring out the worst in me and not only because she didn't even greet her only child. If anything, she wished we weren't here at all, and I hurt for Abi more than myself.

"That wasn't part of the agreement."

"Shit happens." I speak, loving how her mother winces at the hard edge of my words.

If they thought I would be begging for acceptance, they've got another thing coming and the only begging to be done is their forgiveness for treating their daughter this way.

"Judge Stevenson is arranging an annulment and nothing more will be said about it. You will leave." He stares at me with an autocratic glare and then flicks a look of disappointment at his daughter, who just squeezes my hand even tighter.

"I understand you are blackmailing Jefferson Stevenson." He turns his sneer onto me, and I shrug. "It happens when someone steps out of line. I'm sure you have used similar tactics yourself, Jared, and I'm guessing you're about to use them again."

He recoils a little, probably not used to anyone speaking back and firing off truths like bullets into the room.

"Possibly, but my manipulation isn't for criminal purposes."

"Are you sure about that?"

I fix him with my deadliest stare and snarl, "You had your reasons for allowing Abigail to walk away with me. I was surprised that you never even put up a fight and just allowed it to happen."

"You gave me no choice." He snaps and I laugh out loud. "Don't treat me like a fool, Jared. If anything, you think I am one."

I lean forward and stare at them both long and hard. "I'm guessing it was to rid yourself of a problem that only a man like me can carry out."

"I don't know what you are talking about."

He stands firm and I shrug, casting a dismissive gaze at his disapproving wife.

"You wanted me to dispose of Mario Bachini because he was becoming a threat you could no longer ignore. He was going to blow your world apart when he demanded to marry your daughter."

Jared visibly pales and I realize I'm right as I hiss, "You didn't reckon on me taking his place. Making her my wife and ruining your well-orchestrated plan. Marriage to Jefferson would keep them under your control. Your perfect world would continue nicely and there would be no public humiliation in having Mario Bachini as a son-in-law."

He remains frozen and my mind goes into overdrive as I hiss, "Remove the Bachinis from your life and the threat is gone. Abigail and Jefferson will be the golden couple, and you will retain respectability and secure your business for the next generation."

I shake my head. "What I don't understand is your connection to Sam."

I glance at his wife and see the fear in her eyes, and I wonder about that.

"I heard you were an old school friend of his wife."

She flinches but sits straight-backed and stares in front of her as Jared hisses, "Our family history has nothing to do with this. If anything, you're right, because I did want Mario Bachini removed from Abigail's life. She has been groomed to take the highest position in society and that is why you must walk away now, because you will never be accepted into this family."

"Then we will leave now." Abigail stands and faces her father with all guns blazing.

"How dare you?" She hisses and the shock on their faces makes me laugh out loud and I settle back to watch the part of the show when the worm turns.

"I have done everything you wanted. Played by your rules, been the best daughter I could and yet you never gave me any credit for that. If anything, I was just a doll to you. A chess piece to move across the board so you win the game."

She glares between them and says sadly, "You wanted me to marry a man who fucked whores in his spare time. Who didn't love me and treated me like another possession. We had no relationship and were just carrying out your orders and you expect me to be happy about that? To live *your* dream, not mine, just because I owe you for all this somehow."

She waves her hand around her and says sadly, "Is this so important to you that you would sacrifice decency and love? Nothing else matters but the empire you've built on dirty money."

"Abigail!" Anna jumps up and faces her daughter, finally

breaking out from her ice palace and facing her daughter with blazing fury in her eyes.

"We have given you everything. You are a spoiled bitch who needs to learn manners. We are your parents and demand your respect."

I step forward in a flash and catch the arm that threatens to slap her daughter around the face and as I grip it hard, I say roughly, "Nobody touches my wife, ever!"

I push her back and she stumbles beside her husband, who yells, "Enough!"

He turns to Abigail and says sadly, "You are right. We have expected too much from you. But it was done with your best interests at heart."

"My best interests."

Abi shakes her head. "You never asked what I wanted. You don't even know what my best interests are, but I found them out for myself, with Matteo. He loves me."

She smiles and finds my hand and faces her parents, softening her voice.

"I love him. Isn't that worth everything?"

Her mom snarls. "It's worth nothing."

For a moment, the silence settles on the room as if trying to calm the situation and then Abigail says sadly, "Then we will leave, and you will never see us again."

As we turn to walk away, her father says with some desperation.

"OK! I'll tell you."

CHAPTER 36

ABIGAIL

It's as if time stands still as we turn and face the broken soul of a man I always thought was the strongest one I had ever met. Now he looks a shadow of his former self as he sinks down onto the couch and places his head in his hands.

Mom says in shock, "No, Jared!"

He sighs and says softly, "They need to hear it, Anna. This is falling away from us and unless we act now, you can say goodbye to everything we've worked so hard for."

I'm surprised when my mom drops beside him and places her arm around his shoulders and whispers, "You don't have to do this, honey."

I am more shocked at that than anything preceding it, because for once my mother appears almost human.

Matteo guides me back to the couch and places his arm around my shoulder and it's so good knowing I have someone fighting in my corner for once in my life and I say softly, "Tell us what?"

My mother speaks first, which surprises me as she faces me with an expression I've never seen before. Vulnerability.

"I'm sorry, Abigail."

I stiffen because when does my mother ever apologize?

"Everything you said is right, which is why we owe you an apology and an explanation."

She takes a deep breath and whispers, "Your father met Judge Stevenson and Sam Bachini at college. I also went there and became friends with Claire. We all grew close, and I don't think I've ever been as happy as I was back then."

She smiles at the memory and says sadly. "Your father lived in a house with several other guys, and they joined a fraternity called The Dark Lords."

I sit up and share a worried look with Matteo, who is suddenly more alert as we wait for the final puzzle piece to be turned over.

"It was by invitation, and only the richest kids with the most influential parents were allowed to try out. I was so proud when they accepted your father and for a while we enjoyed the status it brought. Then they allowed Sam Bachini to join, and the Dark Lords became a lot more sinister."

She turns to my father and smiles reassuringly. "He is an evil man with evil friends. He held a power nobody could ignore and soon he manipulated your father and the Judge into things that weren't strictly legal. They were tempted by wealth and power, which is the downfall of many great men, and when they all left college, they decided to work together to achieve greater power."

I shiver when I'm faced with the reason behind their success and realize they are no better than Matteo and his family, worse even because it's obvious our billions have been gained from greed and shady deals that probably cost my parents their souls.

My father speaks up. "Sam loved the darker side of life and became a respectable criminal, hiding his crimes behind a charitable institution that opened many doors for him. Judge

Stevenson acted to clear up any mistakes, and I became the business behind the crimes. The respectable face of a world that was anything but. We were so tightly knit it became impossible to break away, and we agreed that to protect our organization, we would unite our families by marrying our children. Conveniently Judge Stevenson had a son, and I had a daughter and everyone's fate was sealed. Then Sam and Claire adopted Mario, and the game changed. He wanted his own son to be the greatest power in the land, and that could only be achieved by respectability. If he married you, Abigail, he would have an open door to Washington's elite, and we would carve his way to power to benefit us all."

Anna nods. "We reminded him that the arrangement had already been made, and Abigail must marry Jefferson but Sam wasn't happy. He told us Mario was standing by as the best choice, and we should cooperate."

"But I stood my ground because the last thing I wanted for you was marriage to a criminal bastard and make no mistake, Mario Bachini is the worst example of that."

Matteo interrupts. "Then she married an even greater one. It's funny how life works out."

Nobody laughs and I say gently, "I fell in love. Is that such a bad thing?"

Mom shakes her head. "No, it's not and I should be happy about that, but it wasn't your decision to make."

"Not my decision! Of course, it was." I am incensed and my father says sadly, "I thought when Sam learned you were with Matteo, he would back off. Fight fire with fire, as they say, and that Matteo would do what I hoped he would."

"Which was?" I say with a hitch to my voice, and he stares at me hard and says roughly, "Remove Mario from our lives."

I glance at Matteo in shock at the realization my father used him, but Matteo merely shrugs, appearing more interested than anything.

"You took a chance I would remove Mario from Abigail's life for what, exactly?"

Mom says quickly, "We wanted him gone. He was too volatile, too corrupt and threatened our whole organization."

"The Dark Lords?" I'm confused, hating knowing my father is involved in that, but if anything, my father seems confused.

"The Dark Lords were a fraternity, Abigail. We left it behind in college."

Matteo hisses, "Then why do you have the fucking rule book hidden in a drawer in your penthouse?"

My father is incensed as he yells, "You broke into my apartment!"

Matteo shrugs. "I did what was necessary to protect your daughter. Something you are obviously incapable of."

I stare in bewilderment at a scene I wasn't expecting and I'm even more surprised when my father says with a sigh, "It's complicated."

"So you *are* involved." I stare at him in horror and he sighs heavily.

"Yes, I'm involved but not in the way you think."

"Then how?"

He glances at my mother and appears almost ashamed. "I abide by the rules but don't attend any meetings. I've spent a lifetime trying to distance myself from my involvement but I understand things happen I have control over. As far as I know the Dark Lords is just a club that protects its members and pushes opportunities their way to help them get on in life."

Matteo shakes his head. "Then tell that to Mario and his real father, who is apparently the Supreme Dark Lord, or some shit like that."

"His father?"

I stare in shock as my parents share a horrified look and my father says in a low whisper, "You heard about him?"

I brazen it out and say firmly, "We know Sam isn't Mario's real father. Jefferson told us, but we don't know his name."

My father stands and appears agitated and says roughly, "Then leave it that way. Walk away and forget you heard anything at all."

He appears almost possessed as he stares at me with blind panic and says to Matteo. "If you feel anything for my daughter, you will walk away now. Let her marry Jefferson and live a safe and happy life. If she leaves with you, you will both end up dead. If anything, I can promise you that."

Matteo jumps up and snarls. "I want his name."

My father says defiantly, "I will *never* speak his name. I will do anything to protect my family and you will never get it from me. If Abigail leaves with you, she may as well be committing suicide."

Mom turns to me and her usual composure crumbles as she says, "Please, Abigail. Stay here where we can protect you."

I stare at Matteo in shock and the only sound other than my own frantic breathing is a text coming through on his phone and I watch his expression change to one of pure rage when he reads it.

He glances up, and if anything, the look he directs at my parents is one of controlled rage as he hisses, "Request denied. Say goodbye to your parents, Abigail, because the safest place for you is by my side."

I stare at my parents in shock, as Matteo says in a voice laced with pain, anger and retribution.

"This ends now."

CHAPTER 37

MATTEO

I am so angry I want to tear this mansion apart. Of course it's him. The fucking bastard. The most important thing right now is to head home and inform my brothers because we don't have long before shit gets very real. Jefferson's slate has been wiped clean, but I doubt he'll survive long enough to enjoy it if word gets out he betrayed Mario's father. Now it's up to me and my brothers to end this shit once and for all.

I am surrounded by red fury as I drag Abi away from her protesting parents and step out into the sunlight, my soldiers crowding around us as a barrier against her parents, who shout, "Abigail, please, don't do this."

Abi is shaking as she slides into the car before me and her pale face peers at me with concern as the door slams behind me.

"What is it?"

"It's important we return home."

"No. The text. What did it say?"

"It's business, Abi!" I yell at her because I will not bring her into this. She needs to be protected, and that includes blissful ignorance and so I say roughly, "My business is not yours."

"Like fuck it is!" She yells and I turn and grip her by the throat, hating the alarm that sparks in her eyes as I hiss, "Don't push me, princess, because you won't like the man I become when business is involved. Go home, catch up on some sleep, and leave me to do what I do best."

I release her and turn my attention to my phone, any earlier happiness destroyed by just one name and as Abigail shrinks away from me, I can't even deal with the pain that creates inside me because I would rather she hate me, than live with the fear of what's coming.

She is my number one priority, and I will *not* involve her in this. If I'm sure of anything, it's that and to protect what we have I must focus on business now. When I saw that name, I realized shit was getting real, and it struck me that since meeting Abi, I've never had so much to lose.

I dash out the appropriate text, and as we reach the jet, I waste no time. Abi takes her seat by the window and pointedly looks away, which suits me fine because it's Cesare I need right now.

Most of the flight is spent speaking in hushed whispers and working out strategy because I'm under no illusions at all that we need a plan and fast.

I don't even think about Abi fuming at the front of the aircraft. I don't have that luxury because time is not on our side.

The one time I take a break, I move to her side, almost like a magnetic pull, and when I see her sleeping peacefully, my heart beats with so much love for my pretty princess. She sits curled up on the seat and without thinking, I reach for a blanket and drape it over her body, wishing like hell I could pull her into my arms and hold on tight. I've never wanted to protect anyone so much in all my life as this woman who has crashed into my world and blown it apart. She is everything to me and my reaction earlier was driven by fear—for her. I won't lose her as soon as I've found her, but I must face the possibility it could happen.

For a good few minutes, I sit and watch her, savoring the sight of a woman who is so far out of my league it still shocks me that she is here at all.

I reluctantly tear my eyes from her and head back to business and as we discuss strategy, my mind wanders back to the front of the plane. I nearly lost her once, but I'm aware the battle isn't over yet. If anything, the danger has increased because I have killed the son of a bastard and he won't rest until he makes me pay.

We land and the usual cars are waiting and as soon as Abi is safely beside me and the door closes, I sigh heavily and say apologetically, "I'm sorry, princess."

She shrugs and looks down at her twisted hands and I hate the distance that has grown between us, which is entirely of my own making.

Reaching out, I cover her hand with mine and say gently, "What happened back there was a reaction. The most important thing in my life is to keep you safe. The name I saw doesn't keep any of us safe and the least you know of it, the better."

"You don't trust me." She turns and the pain in her eyes makes me feel like the biggest bastard on the planet and I shake my head. "Of course I trust you. It's the rest of them I don't."

I try to make a joke, but she isn't laughing and neither, as it happens, am I.

I twist her face to mine and whisper against her lips, "You must let me protect you in the best way I can. Ignorance is bliss and I want you to be happy knowing I am in your corner fighting for you — for us."

I sigh and whisper, "When this is over, I will take you away.

A honeymoon of sorts and we can relax without glancing over our shoulders, wondering if we'll make it through the day."

"Is it really that bad?"

I hate the worry that clouds her beautiful eyes and I smile gently. "Not if we make the first move. It's why we had to leave so I can meet up with my brothers and mark out our battle lines."

"Are you in danger?" She looks so worried I lie to her. "Worry about the rest of them, princess. Nothing can touch me."

She raises her eyes and I grin cockily. "Self belief. Try it, I recommend it."

She blinks away the tears and surprises me by crushing her lips to mine and, just like that, my heart is right back where I want it to be.

I don't believe my lips leave hers for the entire journey. It's not even sexual, not this time. It's a promise, a declaration and a desperation that I have passed on to my wife. Everything could change because of one man, and I have never felt so vulnerable, but I'm an Ortega and we don't let shit happen without putting up a damned good fight.

* * *

We reach my penthouse back in New York and as soon as we step inside, I turn to Abi and say gently, "You'll be safe here. Settle back in, sleep, eat and rest. I won't be long."

"Where are you going?"

"The club."

"Please don't leave me." She looks panicked and inside I share that emotion but outwardly I remain calm and say firmly, "Nothing can hurt you here, princess. This is a gold lined fortress and is the best place for you now. Nobody will come in and nobody can get out. I have security measures set up, and my soldiers will protect you with their lives. Stephanie is down the hall and if you need company, I'm guessing she would appreciate it. Just stay here until I return. I won't be long."

I pull her toward me with an urgent need to feel her lips on mine, just one taste before my mind sets to business.

I'm not afraid for Abi, not here in my home because I have done everything possible to make it impenetrable.

She clings onto me as if she can't bear to let me go and I sigh and pull away, smiling my reassurance.

"A couple of hours tops, then I'll need to unwind, and the best place for that is my dungeon."

I wink, loving the flush on her face when I remind her of a place we have yet to experience and the desire that lights in her eyes makes me smile. Yes, my girl is a lady on the outside and a whore inside, and I still can't believe how I got so lucky.

CHAPTER 38

ABIGAIL

I'm not sure what to think anymore. Things changed in the blink of an eye when Matteo received that text and the speed of our exit left me breathless. I can't even imagine what startled him so much, but it was as if a bomb detonated in the room.

I'm still reeling from seeing my parents and what they told me. They have been hiding secrets from me my entire life and I wonder if I would ever have discovered them if it hadn't been for Matteo.

I wander into the apartment and stare through the floor length window at a view I will never grow tired of. My entire world has changed, and it's because of one man. The hardened criminal who I fell head over heels in love with. I am not thinking straight at all where he is concerned and yet something is telling me he has more honor in his pinkie than my parents have in their entire bodies combined. He puts me first, which is something they have never done, and it hardens my heart against them, bringing my loyalty firmly down on his side.

A small movement behind me makes me spin in surprise, and I see Stephanie hovering nervously in the doorway.

"I'm sorry, I'll…"

"No." I smile away my concern. "Please, come and join me. I could use some company."

She smiles nervously and heads into the room and I say with a grin, "We should discover what passes as a kitchen in this place. I could murder a coffee."

"It's through there." She points to a door leading to a hallway. "Come. I became familiar with this place when you all left. I'll fix you a coffee and something to eat if you like."

I nod and follow her out of the room and stare with interest at a space that is much bigger than I first thought. The hallway leads to another large landing where a staircase heads down and at the bottom is another one with rooms leading off it.

I love this place. It's so chic and elegant but has a cosiness that appears at odds with what I know about Matteo and as we head into a large modern kitchen, I stare around me in wonder.

"This is impressive."

Stephanie nods. "It is. This whole apartment is amazing. I've had a good poke around and I never want to leave."

I stare at her with a burning curiosity. "Tell me about you and Cesare."

At the mention of her man, her whole face lights up and as she reaches for the kettle, she sighs wistfully. "I met him at Mr. Ortega's club where I worked after college. I found him scary but he had something that appealed to me."

She grins, making me laugh out loud because I definitely recognize that appeal and she grins as she sets about her task. "I never dared speak to him or to any of them. We could look but never approach, unless bringing them drinks or at their request. I looked a lot, though. I found it impossible not to, and Cesare was the man I looked at the most. He was so dark, so dangerous, and closed off to everyone around him. Almost as if he was in his own head space and withdrew from the shit that surrounds them all."

"Shit?"

She nods. "The women mainly, all desperate to be noticed. I tried to disguise my interest because I didn't want to be labeled as one of them."

She pushes the mug of coffee across the counter toward me and sits beside me on a bar stool.

"I sensed his eyes on me, though. Watching me as I worked and studying my movements. Some would call it creepy. I loved it."

"What happened next?"

I'm enthralled by her story, and she laughs softly. "One night, I was cleaning up at closing time. Mr. Ortega was working, and Cesare came into the club for a bottle of whiskey. He moved behind the bar to take one from the shelf and backed me up against the counter as he reached past me. He appeared in no hurry to leave and stared into my eyes with that dark gaze that brought me immediately to my knees and before I could even react, he kissed me so passionately I swear I didn't breathe once the entire time."

"Wow. That's so hot." My eyes are wide as she reminds me our men take what they want as if it's their right and for some reason that is acceptable because of who they are.

"I swear I couldn't have told him to stop if I wanted to and I didn't. If anything, I *never* wanted him to stop."

"Then what happened?"

She looks a little shame faced. "He pulled away and stroked my face, his dark eyes burning into mine and said in that sexy voice that gets me every time, you're coming home with me."

"That's…" I can't even begin to describe how wrong that is, and she nods, laughing out loud. "Arrogant. I'm positive Cesare invented that word because he didn't even ask. He never has and despite the fact I wanted to go with him so badly, I turned him down."

"Wow, way to go, Stephanie, you've got some balls."

She grins. "Outwardly, but inside I was a hot mess. I wanted to go so badly, but I didn't intend on falling in line like every other woman before me and I'm guessing there were many."

"Guessing?"

"I never actually saw him with anyone else. None of them, really. For hot men in a candy store, they appeared impervious to the lap dancers and many women who stopped by their table. They were the untouchables. Look but don't touch, in public, anyway."

"So, there weren't any women. I find that hard to believe." I shake my head because there is no way in hell I believe that.

She shakes her head. "Oh, there were women alright. Ones they paid for a few hours and then sent packing. It made me determined never to be one of them and I heard the stories of the society women who yearned to be even noticed by them. That's what I was fighting against because despite the fact I worked as a waitress in a lap dancing club, I never performed. My clothes stayed on, and I had the protection of security because my sole purpose was to keep the customers' glasses full."

"What did Cesare say when you turned him down?"

I'm intrigued, and she rolls her eyes.

"He didn't accept my answer. He merely gripped my wrist hard and repeated, 'you are coming with me whether you like it or not' and he swept me up into their world like a tornado passing by and carrying me along with it."

She grins, her eyes lit with so much love for the enigmatic man she calls her own, and says with a smile, "He took me to another penthouse across town. It's where Mr. Ortega conducts business and I never knew this place existed until he brought me here after…" She shivers and gulps a shot of caffeine before saying, "Anyway. He took me there and within twenty-four hours, I fell hopelessly in love with him. He was nothing like I imagined and made me feel so special, I would have done anything for him. I still would."

"How did you, um...?"

"End up with Mario?"

Stephanie shivers. "Cesare went out of town on business. It was common, and he was away more than at home. By then we were an item and from that first night, inseparable. I worked in the club occasionally, but only because I insisted and only when he was there. It was his only concession, and I wasn't about to argue with him because it wouldn't have ended well. Anyway, that day I headed out for some fresh air. I went jogging around Central Park most days and even though Cesare always made me take a protection team to jog behind me, I foolishly decided I wanted to be normal for once and slipped out alone. I knew it wouldn't be long before they found me, it almost became a game of mine testing how long it took them to appear by my side, so when two men jogged up close behind me, I never gave them a second look."

I stare at her with concern as her face falls, and she gulps, "We turned the corner, and they pressed a gun into my back and told me to come quietly and not to make a scene. The fact it was early, and nobody was even around, made that statement ridiculous, but I didn't ignore the terror inside as I was guided toward a waiting car on the edge of the park. The door opened, and they pushed me inside, where Mario was waiting."

She turns and the expression in her eyes sickens me as she says in a sad voice. "Before I could scream, he injected me with something and I woke up on that fucking stone altar in his house of horror."

I reach out and cover her hand with mine, squeezing it reassuringly as the tears slide down her face.

"The rest you can kind of guess. It wasn't pleasant, and he

broke me. I realized the only way to survive was to play the game until the opportunity arose to escape. I never thought that would happen though, because we were treated like animals and chained up when not in use. Many girls fought and paid a heavy price, but I worked smart and soon gained their trust of sorts. I was allowed more freedom to clean and maintain the cleanliness of the mansion, and that was a lot of help to pass the time. I didn't fight them in the obvious way, but I planned my escape almost every fucking hour."

"I will never be able to thank you enough for helping me that day." I say with heartfelt thanks, and she smiles.

"I was happy to help someone escape from the madness. Diana visited sometimes without Mario. Occasionally, she would come and check up on things, usually before another ceremony. Making sure everything was ready and perfect because Mario expected it. He would fly into a rage if he found just one thing out of place, and I figured she was just making certain he remained happy. Then she surprised me by telling me that Mario would bring a woman here and make her his wife. My job was to stop that from happening."

She sighs. "I was so afraid and wondered if they were testing me, but Diana showed me the way to the tunnels and told me what to do. I had only ever been the hunted before and never realized there were exits embedded in the walls, which made sense when Mario sometimes appeared in front of me rather than behind. It became his own personal playroom, and he liked to play a lot. He would give you a head start and then taunt you with fear as he got closer and closer, using his whip to bring you down and then using it to punish you for running in the first place."

"The fucking bastard." I remember only too well what that felt like, and I can only imagine the horror of what happened when he caught up with the poor woman running for her life.

"It was hell on earth living there." Stephanie's eyes are

clouded with pain, and she shivers. "Rape, torture and beatings that took you to the edge of life. Orgies and pain became common place in our world. He liked to steal a woman from the street and lock them away for his own personal pleasure and I still don't know to this day if he knew who I was, or just saw his chance one misty day in Central Park."

"Matteo told me that Cesare was destroyed when you left."

She nods sadly. "I was so worried he would think I had run away. I had fallen so deeply in love with him he was all I could think of, and that memory kept me alive because I had someone worth fighting for."

I smile and inject some brightness into my voice. "I'm glad you got your happy ending. You're back together. We all are."

She nods, a wistful smile on her face, and it strikes me how incredibly beautiful she is. I'm not surprised that Cesare fell hard for this woman because there's an innocence and fragility that surrounds her that would ignite the protective streak in any man.

"It's good to be home." She smiles and then says with a shake of her head. "Anyway, why don't we enjoy the time we have without our men and order takeout and watch movies? There's a fucking cinema in this penthouse that you will die for."

"Sounds good to me." And it does. Being here suits me just fine, and any fears I had are pushed firmly away. Matteo is my everything, much like Cesare is Stephanie's, and a life with these people is way more attractive than the one I was facing a short time ago, no matter how long that will be. Surely a few months spent with the right person are worth decades with the wrong one. If that's all we get, then I'm up for the ride because I have a feeling it's going to be a wild one and I can't fucking wait.

CHAPTER 39

MATTEO

I reach the club and once again I am plunged headfirst into darkness. This is my world. Shrouded in pain, violence and dirty money. It drips from the walls and reminds me who I am. Abi is the only light in my world and it's no wonder I crave it like a drug because it's the only glimmer of hope I have of surviving the shit I deal with daily.

They are waiting in my office, and my heart thumps as I prepare to meet my brothers for the first time since we left a few years ago.

Cesare is quiet beside me as he senses I'm too worked up to talk and as we reach my office, he says gruffly, "I'll be down the hall. Call me if you need me."

I nod, wishing I had the luxury of escaping this meeting, but this is probably the most important one of my life and as I head inside, two identical pairs of eyes stare at me for the first time in what feels like forever. I'm surprised at the emotion in them as my brothers stand.

For a second they regard me warily and the tension in the room is so thick it's difficult to battle through it and then I say with a sigh, "It's good of you to come."

Dom nods and Leo says drily, "We had no choice."

I nod, a sinking feeling telling me there is a long way to go before we're one big happy family, not that we ever were and as we take our seats, I am itching for the nicotine my cigar provides but settle for a shot of whiskey to calm my nerves.

Leo glares through his usual enigmatic eyes and growls, "I have news of my own."

We stare at him expectantly and he says gruffly, "I read the will."

This *is* news and Dom growls, "It had better be in our fucking favor."

Leo laughs bitterly. "What do you think?"

"Tell us." I growl, knowing I'm not going to like what's in it, knowing immediately Diana will be named as head of this family.

"Carlos Matasso."

"What about him?"

I raise my eyes and Leo snaps. "The person inheriting the Ortega empire is Carlos Matasso."

It's as if he's launched a grenade in the room and we dive for cover while we wait for the dust to settle, because I'm not sure either of us can believe what we're hearing.

Dom speaks first and shouts, "What the actual fuck? You had better be wrong."

"I'm not." Leo sighs. "I saw it written for myself. Giovanni Ortega's last will and testament names Carlos Matasso as the sole beneficiary of his estate. There weren't even any bequests. He gets the lot. We are now out of business or dead."

I say with a deep sigh. "It all makes sense."

"I'm glad you think so." Dom growls, and I say with a sigh, "The reason I called this meeting is to tell you that Mario is dead but it leaves us with a huge problem."

They stare at me with cold fury, and I nod. "He was into some dark lord shit and kidnapped Abi and I went after her and hung him from his depraved neck. Diana told me where to find him and got us into the fucking house of hell, but slipped away when shit got real."

"Diana helped you to kill Mario?"

Dom looks shocked and Leo leans back in his seat with a low, "Fuck me."

For a second, we let the information sink in and then I tell them the reason they're here in the first place.

"The problem is, Sam Bachini wasn't Mario's father. He was adopted."

"And?" Leo stares at me hard and I growl, "That pleasure belongs to Carlos Matasso."

"Fuck!" Dom yells and Leo's eyes glisten with rage as he shakes his head slowly before saying with a low growl. "Then it's even more important to change direction."

"What do you mean?" We stare at him expectantly, and he leans back and regards us through his usual emotionless eyes.

"We change the will and kill Matasso before he even knows we're on to him."

"What with? Harry fucking Potter's cloak of invisibility?"

Dom scoffs because it's impossible to get anywhere near Carlos Matasso, and we all know that.

Leo peers over at Dom and growls, "Flora."

Dom's head snaps up and his eyes narrow. "What about her?"

"Find out what she knows about the Matassos. She lived with them long enough; she must be able to tell us something. Spread the word around people you trust not to pass on the information and find out every piece of intelligence you have."

He glances over at me. "Same for you. Get your consigliere onto it and I'll do the same. We need as much information as possible to bring that bastard down."

"We have two fucking days before that fucking will is read."

I say with disgust and Leo shrugs. "I have a plan that will delay that from happening."

"How?" We stare at him with interest, and he grins, telling me my brother has already prepared for this and he says softly, "Ernest Bagway is currently on vacation. He is due to land tomorrow morning and his cab will be making a detour."

"That's your plan. Lock up the fucking lawyer?" I shake my head.

"It will buy us some time because when he reads that will, it won't be the one our dear father signed."

"You think Ernest Bagway will accept that shit? That man is so straight we would be under investigation in no time."

"You say he's straight. I disagree,"

Leo shrugs. "I haven't been sitting at home waiting for shit to get real. I've been working on this twenty-four seven and I happen to know our father's lawyer is not as pure as he makes out."

"What have you got on him?"

I'm mildly interested, and Leo grins. "Rather a lot as it happens and I'm certain he will turn a blind eye to this one indiscretion in return for my silence because it's that or life imprisonment."

"Wow, what's the fucker done?"

Leo just smiles. "Things no man wants to admit in prison. Ernest Bagway is about to learn a valuable lesson and the payment will be his silence in return for ours."

I nod. "But that doesn't mean we're off the hook with Matasso. I'm guessing he already knows that I murdered his son and is already planning retribution."

Leo shrugs. "It's doubtful he will do anything until the will is read. Once he has the Ortega mafia, he will strike, but only then. The delay means we have longer to react to that and every man has an Achilles heel."

"Then I hope you've fucking found his." I say with a sigh

and Leo nods, looking quite smug for once, making us stare at him expectantly.

"There is one woman who hates him more than we do, and I know where she is hiding."

"That's your plan, a woman?" Dom huffs with exasperation.

Leo shrugs. "Never underestimate the power of a woman, brother. Look what happened the last time we did that."

He reminds us all of the traitor that currently sits at the head of this family and Dom says with interest, "Who is she?"

"The daughter of a woman Carlos murdered several years ago. She wants her revenge and has been sharpening her skills accordingly."

Dom sighs, "You are seriously thinking a woman can fix this. She had better be a fucking warrior with a fucking army, because that's what we need."

"Trust me brothers. She is our best shot, so leave me to unleash the beast and concentrate on gathering information."

He stands and, as always, it makes me lower my eyes because even from an early age, Leo commanded respect. He doesn't have the brute force of Dom or the hunger for violence. He doesn't revel in information gathering like I do, but he is the man who gets shit done. He has an aura of darkness that sucks the oxygen from any room and keeps any thoughts or emotions well hidden behind his enigmatic eyes.

He is the most dangerous one of us because when it comes to Leo, you never know what he's thinking and his thoughts aren't for the faint hearted and as enemies go, Carlos Matasso has just made an extremely dangerous one in Leonardo Ortega.

CHAPTER 40

ABIGAIL

The door clicks open, and I close my eyes tightly, pretending to be asleep to resist the urge I have to run to him. When he left earlier, for a moment, it was as if I was having a panic attack. It soon passed, but it struck me how dependant I am on him in such a short space of time, and I don't like it. What if he tires of me clinging to him and suffocating him?

Before I met him, I like to think I was an independent woman, in thought only that is. I was strong, and able to hide my emotions, which protected me, kind of, anyway. All my life, I've hidden behind a façade of superiority and a coolness that's served me well. The ice queen, I suppose, not the desperate woman Matteo Ortega has made me into.

The more time I spend with him, the harder I'm falling and when I hit the ground, I know I will break. For now, he is intrigued by me, but that could soon turn to indifference, so I decided to make myself stronger just to stand a chance of keeping his love.

I'm not even sure what the future holds for us. We are married, but for how long? If my father gets his way, it was just a ceremony that will be banished to the history books and swept under the rug as my dirty little secret. I will be made to marry someone like Jefferson to try to gather the remaining tatters of respectability that my family are clinging onto. I know how this all works. I'm not a fool and worlds like mine and the Ortega's are never permitted to collide.

So, I need to prepare for that and try to distance myself from my husband because I have a sinking feeling that privilege is a fleeting one and sooner rather than later, I'll be back where I started—alone.

The bed dips and I half turn away, trying desperately to remain indifferent, and then a rough hand traces a light path down my body, pushing my thighs apart and caressing my clit. My eyes snap open because, for fuck's sake, this is so unfair and the lustful eyes that stare back at me cause a shiver of excitement to ripple through my body.

"Honey, I'm home." He whispers close to my ear, and I gasp as his finger enters my pussy and pushes in deep. His thumb caresses my clit, and I can't prevent the low moan that escapes, telling him in an instant that he's won this particular battle, and the smirk on his face makes me angry with myself for falling at the first fucking hurdle.

He carries on, staring into my eyes and working my body until the pressure increases and my breath comes in short, needy pants. My body arches toward his hand, desperate to be played by a professional and I must give him praise. He's genius at what he does.

Just when I think he's broken me, he removes his finger and places it into his mouth, sucking it clean as he stares at me with so much lust, I catch my breath.

"Come."

He reaches for my hand, and I stare up at him in confusion as he says almost roughly, "There's something I need to show you."

"But…" I hate that I sound needy and slightly petulant because he has denied me something he promised the moment he touched my body and the spark in his eyes intrigues me as he says with a wicked smile, "It's time to erase memories."

Despite the fact I haven't got a clue what he's talking about, something is telling me it's for my benefit, so I follow him from the room, dressed only in a silk chemise, wondering if I should change.

He doesn't appear to care that I'm almost naked and as we leave his bedroom, he walks the short distance to the room he showed me on the first day I was here. The room that intrigued me then and fills me with apprehension now.

His dungeon.

We reach the door, and my heart rate increases as with no words, he lifts the silk from my body, so I stand naked before him. The fact he is still fully dressed all in black makes my mouth water because there is something so incredibly sexy about the dark and dangerous man staring at me with lustful intent, promising me I'm about to learn what the word pleasure really means.

He stands back and runs that wicked gaze the length of me, his desire burning and branding me in a second as his. I will always be his. I'm resigned to that, but how long before he turns that gaze onto a fresh challenge and leaves me to pick up the pieces?

"Trust me, princess."

His command increases my heart rate because what the fuck is he going to do and yet I merely nod and cast my mind back to the first night we met, and he took my virginity in a cold callous act of ownership.

I loved it. I lusted after it because I was the one in control of my body and I was making a decision that was one big fuck you to my parents. We have come full circle now and I know what he's doing. He's gifting ownership back to me by giving me a choice. To anyone looking in, they wouldn't see it that way, but I know what this is. He is giving me what I need.

Freedom.

A slow smile spreads across my face and I nod, feeling the energy rush through my body as I sense I'm about to get the old Abigail Kensington back.

"I trust you, Mr. Ortega. Sir." I smile and his eyes flash with approval as I confirm to him that I have understood exactly what this is.

He nods and pushes the door open and I gasp when I regard the room with only one aim in mind. Depravation and pleasure. Something we shouldn't want. A forbidden desire that reaches out and holds you prisoner because there is nothing quite like the rush it gives you. The last time I was in this position, I sobbed with relief that something had gone I'd been holding onto for someone else. It was preserved as a gift to an undeserving recipient, and back then I decided it was mine to give, not my parents. I tossed it aside like an unwelcome albatross around my neck to the first stranger I met. However, fate had its own agenda and gave me a different path to tread, and I suppose I'm at that crossroads when I decide whether I want to stay on it now.

Matteo says darkly, "Walk to the bench and lie face down in the position I found you in that night at the Banned Room.

I nod, my heart thumping with anticipation as he takes us right back where we started.

I assume the position, my cheek resting against the cold leather, my ass high in the air as it waits for his attention. This feels so wicked, so wrong and yet so incredibly right because we have rewound our story to the beginning and the next page is a blank one that only we can script.

The sound of a zipper lowering is like a gunshot in the room, and I tense as he presses against my pussy from behind.

The anticipation is high as I wait for the pleasure to hit me, and I groan out loud as he caresses my ass and then drops to his knees and licks my clit from behind.

I am so wet already, desperate even, and as he teases my sex, I am more irritated than anything else. I just want him to own me, to thrust inside hard and fast and drive out the demons that linger there, making me forget they ever existed,

I want him to take me in a desperate act because that is exactly how I feel now. My legs shake as my body battles to fend off the pleasure he is creating because I want it to be raw with no emotion guiding me.

It's almost as if he's telepathic because he stands and then lands a sharp blow to my ass, causing it to sting like crazy, and I yell out in pain, falling forward on the bench. Then, before I can react, he cuffs my wrists in the smooth metal that hangs either side of the leather bench.

I shouldn't want this, not after what I saw at Mario's fuck house, but this is different. This is on my terms with a man who only has my best interests at heart, and he is demonstrating that now. He gets me. He understands what I need and as another blow hits me hard, I scream into the leather, strangely loving how liberating this experience is.

Then he pulls me back by the hair, like he did the very first time, and growls, "Tell me who owns you, princess."

"You do, sir."

"Who am I?"

He growls close to my ear, and I smile as I say softly, "My husband, sir."

He increases the pressure on my head, causing the desire to drip from my body like a leaking tap because I want him so badly I can't think straight.

My husband. The hard, devastatingly attractive warrior who has brought me under his wicked spell and as he kicks my legs apart and holds me in one hand, he thrusts roughly inside, causing me to cry out as he fucks me hard.

It's brutal and an act of ownership that makes my heart burst. This is what I love. Him inside me doing what he does best. Owning me, loving me and protecting me and I would trust him with my life.

This is exactly what I needed to bring me home and the soft loving can wait while I adjust to my new situation.

The moment I saw Jefferson on his knees, crawling after a whore, it unlocked a side of me that understood exactly why he loved it. It's a release from respectability, giving us a freedom we don't usually enjoy, and I have this man tearing into my body to thank for that. He showed me an open door, and I ran through it, leaving my inhibitions behind. There is nothing more powerful than a woman who opens her mind and takes what she wants and to hell with what's perceived acceptable. Who cares about that when the caged animal inside you is begging to be set free?

Matteo rips through my body like a cyclone and steals every part of resistance I have. I surrender entirely to him and am rewarded with a sensation that takes me to Nirvana. I float back to earth on a cloud of happiness that only he can provide and as he explodes inside me with a dominant roar, this time I'm not left sobbing and broken. This time I am invincible.

CHAPTER 41

MATTEO

We are right back where we started. A clean slate and a promise to walk hand in hand into whatever future we have left.

As I pull out of my wife, I love the red ass that is pointed in my direction. She has slumped on the bench, but this time I'm certain it's with a smile on her face. I knew that the most important thing was to wipe the memories of what happened in Mario's house. She must not fear what happened back there. She made it back and will continue on her own terms. Bringing her back to the beginning demonstrated that life can turn full circle, and you have survived. There will be many challenges along the next turn of that circle, but it will always bring us back to this point. Abi is my wife and that will never change. Now I've found her she is going nowhere without me by her side.

As she lies panting before me, I discard my own clothes in haste because she may think this is over, but she's definitely mistaken about that.

I remove the cuffs, massaging her wrist and pressing my

lips to the burn, loving how her skin flares red because of my touch.

I am a dominant male; I make no apologies for that and as I scoop her into my arms, her lustful gaze makes mine deepen in my eyes.

"Ready for more, princess?"

She smiles with a radiance that catches my breath and withholds the oxygen, causing me to stare in wonder at the most perfect woman I have ever met.

My woman.

The one I never realized existed, but knowing she is in my arms gives me more power than I ever thought possible.

I lead her across to the wall and say roughly, "Remember, trust me. This is for your own good." She appears nervous but nods, her anxiety obvious as she stares at the restraints on the cold stone wall.

I turn her to face me and slip her wrists into the metal cuffs for the second time, and then do the same with her ankles until she is spread out before me.

Her nervous smile unhinges my locked heart because how is she so beautiful and trusting when it's obvious she is shit scared?

"Trust me." I growl and hear her gasp when I reach for the whip that hangs nearby.

"Matteo, I..." She starts to tremble as I crack it against the ground, the sound of it causing her to cry, "Please, no."

The tears slide down her face as she breaks apart as she faces something that will steal the sleep from her body until she faces it.

"I told you to trust me." I growl, hating that I have turned this moment into terror and with a flick of my wrist, I catch her skin with the edge of the tail. Her startled surprise melts the last frozen piece of my heart as a smile ghosts her lips and she whispers, "How?"

I flick the whip again and she shivers as it caresses her body.

"It doesn't hurt."

She gazes at me in wonder, and I nod, guarding against the emotion that is threatening to reveal how much she owns my soul.

"It can." I shrug and grin wickedly. "This whip can be soft and caressing like the most attentive lover, or it can be cruel and unforgiving in the hands of a sadist. It's up to you to decide which one you prefer and there is not just one setting, it can react to your needs."

"I love it." Her eyes shine as I give her more, the tail caressing her body, causing her to groan.

Watching her is the biggest turn on. Spread out before me and loving the effects of something I can do. I fine tune her body until she is ready and as I end this session with a harder flick of the wrist, she screams as her orgasm tears through her, the pain releasing the demon from inside her as she banishes the ghosts of the past.

I can't restrain myself and in two steps push inside her and fuck her hard, loving how her slick walls caress my hard cock as I take what I want, knowing she got there first.

I will never tire of my wife. I know that already and we will explore life together in all its depraved beauty, knowing that we only have our best interests at heart.

We drive one another to the point of exhaustion and finish up on the terrace, wrapped in a blanket, staring into the fire pit. The moon beams its approval down on us and as I hold my princess in my arms, I have never felt so happy.

"What happens next, Matteo?"

She is curious and I wish I knew the answer to that, and I say with a sigh.

"We do whatever is necessary to win."

"Win?" She's confused and I sigh.

"Have you ever heard the name Carlos Matasso?"

She shakes her head and stares up at me with perplexity.

"No, should I?" That makes me feel better at least and I drop a light kiss on her tempting lips and then say with a hard sigh, "He is Mario's father."

She stiffens and I rub her arm almost with distraction.

"It turns out he's also the beneficiary of my father's last will and testament and if everything goes his way, can add the name Don Ortega to his many other titles, the main one being controlling evil bastard."

"What does that mean for you? For us?" She sounds worried, and I try to remain unfazed. "It means we are a problem he needs to deal with."

"Are we in danger?"

"Not yet."

"Yet?"

She shivers and I tighten my hold and growl, "We have a plan, but it's not watertight. Things could go badly wrong and if that happens, I'm sending you back to your father because that is the safest place for you right now."

"NO!" she yells angrily, which makes me smile.

"My place is with you, Matteo. Whether it's here or in the afterlife, I'm sticking by your side."

Abi can't possibly know how deep her words cut because nobody has ever put me before them in my life. It causes an emotion I've never experienced to be released from its cage, because how can I not react to that?

Gripping her face, I stare into her eyes and say firmly, "I love you, Abi, so hard it physically hurts."

Her eyes widen and she stares at me with so much love shining in her eyes, it causes an ache in my heart that has never been there before.

"I love you so much, Matteo. I will never leave you; not for anything. Whatever threatens us, we face it together, and that is non-negotiable."

I nod. The smile that breaks out across my face is solely for her because she makes me so happy I would promise her anything.

I lean forward and whisper against her lips, "As soon as this is over, I'm taking you on our honeymoon to make babies."

"Babies?"

She shakes her head. "One at a time, please."

Her laughter makes me smile and I stroke her cheek lightly. "Babies. I want an army of children that looks just like their mom so I can surround myself with your image every turn I make. They will be loved, protected and happy and so will you, my princess. You have my word on that."

She smiles, and it's as if the moon is dull in comparison and then she whispers, "Why wait until the honeymoon? There is nothing I love more than when you are inside me. Whatever comes for us, we will be prepared, but let's not waste any more time worrying about that. Fuck me like you love me and let's create our own idyllic world."

No more words are needed because we are imagining the same future. We have arrived at our happy ending, even if fate has other ideas.

I must take my own advice and trust my brother because it's now up to Leonardo to save our family and get rid of our enemies and I almost pity Carlos Mattasso because the last man I would want coming for me is the true heir of the Ortega Mafia and if anyone can guarantee our future, it's him.

EPILOGUE

LEO

There are women and there's Chastity Blake. She is the most delicious surprise, certainly unexpected and a challenge I wasn't expecting.

She stares across the table at me with a poker face I would be proud to call my own. She is hiding many secrets behind those enigmatic eyes, and I am the man who is about to reveal them.

I flip my cards and watch for her reaction. There is none. The man to her right sighs in exasperation and throws in his hand, but I don't tear my eyes from hers. The man to her left appears to have given up trying to flirt with her and gives way to anger instead. He stands and throws me a look that would tell most men their lives could be threatened as he retires from the game, leaving a small fortune on the table.

I play to win, but so does my opponent, and she merely turns over her last remaining cards revealing a full house.

There is no triumphant smile and smug joy, just mild curiosity as she waits for my own hand to play.

Without tearing my eyes from hers for a second, I reveal my

own hand and note the disappointment cloud her sexy eyes when I win with a royal flush. To be honest, she has been an unwelcome distraction in a game that requires full concentration before you lose everything.

I'm guessing she is used to that because word on the street is she's unbeaten, until now that is and as she meets my eyes with a wry smile of defeat, she stands and nods to the dealer, pushing her last remaining chips her way as thanks.

I nod to Ryan, my trusted consigliere, to deal with my winnings and I stand, facing the woman who is about to receive an offer she won't be able to refuse and nod toward the bar.

"A word please, Miss. Blake."

If she's surprised that I know her name, she doesn't show it and merely nods as my guards clear a path toward a booth set in the corner of the room, out of sight and unapproachable because I have business to discuss and must not be disturbed.

To her credit, she doesn't react, even with curiosity, which makes me smile. She is a truly gifted poker player and is the one woman I need more than any other right now.

She slips into the booth with no fear at all and as I slide in opposite, I take a moment to stare at a rare beauty. As I heard, she is incomparable because when God created Chastity Blake, it was obvious he couldn't make up his mind.

It's as if every nation is represented in her somehow, from her olive skin, deep brown eyes and long jet-black hair that shines like the purest ebony and flows like silk around her shoulders. She is an enigma and uneasily placed, and yet has a confidence that was sharpened through tragedy. Chastity is the most beautiful and challenging woman I've ever met in my life, and she is gazing at me as if I'm of no consequence at all.

"State your business, Mr. Ortega."

I smile to myself because it's obvious she's done her homework. In fact, I'm guessing she learned the names of every player in the game and has probably done her research accordingly.

"I believe you are two hundred thousand dollars lighter after our last game. I am giving you the opportunity to win it back."

"What does that involve?"

From her expression she's not going to be easily persuaded and probably expects the worse and she should.

"Carlos Matasso."

For the first time, I get a reaction. She tries to disguise it, but her skin pales and her eyes fill with anger and the way she clenches her fist tells me everything I need to know.

"What about him?"

"I believe you have unfinished business concerning him."

"Then you believe wrong, Mr. Ortega. I have no thoughts of him at all. Good day."

She stands, and my guards move closer and seal off any escape she may make, and it almost amuses me to watch her mind calculating if she stands any chance of taking them on.

How I would love to see her try. It would be fascinating to watch. Then again, everything is fascinating about this beauty, and she sits and sighs heavily, her distaste evident on her beautiful face.

"State your business." She fires back at me with a dead expression and a touch of hostility in her voice that she fails to check.

I lean forward and fix her with my darkest stare, loving how she licks her lips and tries to remain in control.

"I need your services."

"Which ones?"

"All of them."

She shakes her head and says dismissively, "Then you will

need a lot more than two hundred thousand dollars, Mr. Ortega."

"I'm offering one million."

I lay out the minimum figure I am prepared to part with and am impressed when she fires back, "Three million."

"Two."

"Done."

There is zero emotion in her voice and certainly none in her expression as she closes a deal before knowing the details.

I reach out and offer her my hand and as hers slips into my larger one, I hold on tightly, knowing that I've won this first battle and as I stare at her full luscious lips, I wonder if the next one will be as easy.

Money is the leveler of many men and I have more of it than most. It's the next part of my plan that may break her, but I'll take this small win while I've got it.

"It begins now." I say darkly, interested in her reaction.

"Then you had better tell me what it involves–" She fixes me with a dark look of her own before saying with a husky voice, "Mr. Ortega."

Now it's my turn to run my tongue along my lower lip because the tension between us is interesting me more than the reason she's here.

I've heard a lot about Chastity Blake, but nothing prepared me for the woman herself, so confident, so composed and an impressive set of skills I would love to own.

"Not here."

"Why not?"

She raises her eyes in a challenge and I feel my eyes glitter as I hiss, "Because I don't discuss business in public, Miss. Blake and I'd be disappointed if you thought it was acceptable."

She nods and as I stand, she does the same and I say firmly, "Until our business is resolved, you remain in my organization.

How long your stay is, is up to you. However, you only have seven days to give me what I want."

"Seven days is a long time, Mr. Ortega."

She raises her eyes, showing none of the fear I would expect from a woman in her position, and I smirk. "Then we are on the same page. Seven days is the target, but feel free to finish the job early, as long as you *do* finish the job, Miss. Blake because, as I said before, you don't get to leave until you do."

The whitening of her skin and the immediate panic in her eyes tells me she has understood exactly what I mean and as she gets her emotion under control, I know we have an understanding.

Chastity Blake has been bought by me for two million dollars and if she fails to deliver, she will *never* leave. Success or death, those are the unspoken rules and now she has an incentive other than money to give me exactly what I want.

Carlos Matasso and his miserable life, or to die trying.

* * *

Thank you for reading The Consigliere. If you want to continue reading Leo's story, click on the link.

Ortega Mafia – The Don

Check out Dom's story
Ortega Mafia – The Enforcer

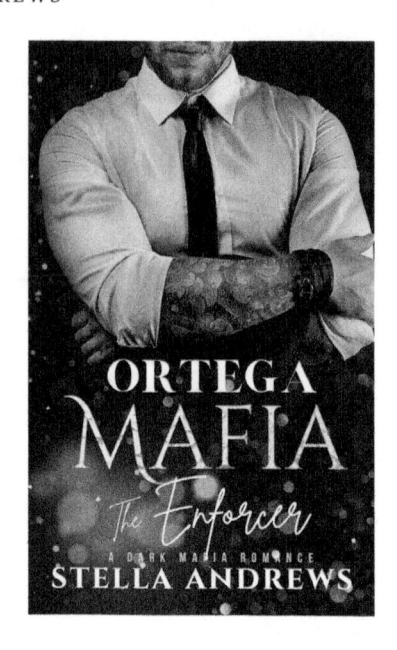

Thank you for reading this story.
If you have enjoyed the fantasy world of this novel, please would you be so kind as to leave a review on Amazon?

Join my closed Facebook Group

Stella's Sexy Readers

Follow me on Instagram

Carry on reading for more Reaper Romances, Mafia Romance & more.

Remember to grab your free book by visiting stellaandrews.com.

ALSO BY STELLA ANDREWS

Twisted Reapers

Sealed With a Broken Kiss
Dirty Hero (Snake & Bonnie)
Daddy's Girls (Ryder & Ashton)
Twisted (Sam & Kitty)
The Billion Dollar baby (Tyler & Sydney)
Bodyguard (Jet & Lucy)
Flash (Flash & Jennifer)
Country Girl (Tyson & Sunny)

The Romanos
The Throne of Pain (Lucian & Riley)
The Throne of Hate (Dante & Isabella)
The Throne of Fear (Romeo & Ivy)
Lorenzo's story is in Broken Beauty

Beauty Series
Breaking Beauty (Sebastian & Angel) *
Owning Beauty (Tobias & Anastasia)
Broken Beauty (Maverick & Sophia) *
Completing Beauty – The series

Five Kings
Catch a King (Sawyer & Millie) *
Slade

Steal a King

Break a King

Destroy a King

Marry a King

Baron

Club Mafia

Club Mafia – The Contract

Club Mafia – The Boss

Club Mafia – The Angel

Club Mafia – The Savage

Club Mafia - The Beast

Club Mafia – The Demon

Ortega Mafia

The Enforcer

The Consigliere

The Don

Standalone

The Highest Bidder (Logan & Samantha)

Rocked (Jax & Emily)

Brutally British

Deck the Boss

Reasons to sign up to my mailing list.

•A reminder that you can read my books FREE with Kindle Unlimited.

•Receive a weekly newsletter so you don't miss out on any special offers or new releases.

•Links to follow me on Amazon or social media to be kept up to date with new releases.

- Free books and bonus content.
- Opportunities to read my books before they are even released by joining my team.
- Sneak peeks at new material before anyone else.

stellaandrews.com

Follow me on Amazon